The Sex Life of a Lagos Mad Woman

'SEUN SALAMI

D1368841

BOOKVINE®

publishability...

ISBN – 978-978-934-077-4

Published in Nigeria by
Bookvine
(Vine Media Services)
14, Adeshina Street, Off Awolowo Way, Ikeja, Lagos, Nigeria.
Tel: +234 803 806 9951, +234 805 569 6965
Email: submissions@bookvineng.com
Website: www.bookvineng.com

This collection of short stories is a work of fiction.
All incidents, people and places in this book are fictional.
Any resemblance to any persons, situations or places is simply coincidental.

To the memory of my late maternal Grandmother,
who I helped lay to rest...

IV

Contents

VI

Breadwinners

KOKUMO, ANYWHERE-BELLE-FACE AND I have been friends from before-before. From the time of stealing dried fish from Kokumo's mother's shop and using it to drink a big bowl of soaked garri together before going to our houses to pretend as if we had not eaten. From the days of tying used clothes together with a rope to make footballs before we were able to start buying cheap rubber balls, putting them into the skin of worn leather balls and blowing the vulcaniser's air into them so that we could feel as if we were really playing leather balls. From the days of going to the fruit seller's shed after sunset to collect all the pieces of fruits cut away from the real ones the rich people had bought.

We collected the fruit remnants in the trash bin as if we were going to help the fruit seller throw his trash away, but when we got to the corner leading to the refuse bin, we settled down and pounced on the bin, the three of us, and chewed and sucked on the sweet juice from whatever remained under each pineapple crown. We scraped out the red lumps under the green peels of pawpaw and sometimes, if it was our lucky day, we even found stale pulps of pawpaws or pineapples or bananas that the fruit seller threw in the trash because to him, they were beginning to rot and rich people never eat rotten fruits. By the time we were done with the trash can, our hands and mouths and shirts were usually stained with mixtures of fruits and we always smelled like we had just been baptised in fruit juice.

We no longer need to steal dried fish or go to the fruit seller's shed anymore because things have changed drastically since we started doing business together: mechanic business, pushing-cars-from-the-highway business, petrol black market business and any other type of business that Anywhere-belle-face brings up. These businesses each have their seasons and we do them as they come. Mechanic business usually goes along with pushing-cars-from-the-highway. Kokumo is a mechanic, even though he did not finish learning from Oga Deinde's workshop. He ran away because the other senior apprentices hated him and always sent him on errands without giving him any tips, so the little he managed to learn is what we use to do the business.

Early in the morning, especially on days that workers go to work in the city, we would go to the highway when traffic must have begun and wait around for cars to break down. We would help to push such cars off the road, make sure they work and then ask the owners to pay us. The bad side of that business is that not everybody that drives a car has money in their pocket. Some people drive cars they borrowed or bought with loans from the money keepers. Some of them would wait until we had suffered to get their cars to work and then start telling us stories of how the government office where they work still owes workers for four good months, or don't we listen to the news?

The best of our businesses was the petrol black market business. No wonder it was the one that finally made us rich. Anytime we heard that there was about to be scarcity of petrol, we knew that we were about to make good money. We would go to the filling station early in the morning before even the attendants arrived and form a queue with our big gallons before the cars began to arrive and formed their own queues. By the time the queues got very long, we would have brought out our gallons of petrol to the road side to sell at almost double the original price. We sold mostly to executive people who couldn't be seen queuing for petrol and did not have time to waste. Those ones who are always looking at their wrists to check the time every few minutes. As good as this business is, it also has a small problem. It is seasonal and you can never know when it will happen except you are like my father who listens to the news all the time; therefore, you cannot depend on it for long, except you get a big breakthrough like us.

My father does not like my business partners, especially Anywhere-belle-face. He thinks he is the one teaching me all the bad-bad things I know because he is the oldest among us. What my father does not know is that I know more bad things than Kokumo and Anywhere-belle-face. He does not even know that I am the one who taught Anywhere-belle-face what to do to Kokumo's sister from the second day he began to catch her under the staircase of their house at night when no one was around. He does not know that I also taught Anywhere-belle-face how to be careful so that he does not get her pregnant like Kokumo's mother's former lover foolishly did to the poor girl. People say she lost the pregnancy even after her tummy had begun to grow bigger than her head because she was still a child herself and therefore couldn't carry a baby successfully. Kokumo does not know about his sister and Anywhere-belle-face. It is not part of our business, it is Anywhere-belle-face's personal love life and I am only his adviser. Even though I am the one who tells him what to do to her, I never ask him to tell me what happened the night before because it is none of my business, as long as he doesn't put her in the family way. That's what my father says whenever we hear that another young girl has become pregnant in the neighbourhood. "Who is the idiot that put such a young girl in the family way?" he would ask my mother, as if he expected her to know the idiot in question. But I always know that things had gone well with Anywhere-belle-face and Kokumo's sister and that he had followed my instructions because of the way he always smiled whenever he saw me the following day.

Anywhere-belle-face got his name from our time of playing football with used clothes tied together like a football. He does not know how to play football because he always kicks the ball wherever his stomach is facing, but he can never agree that he does not know. None of us can tell him that either, because he is bigger than us so we just leave him. Even this name, I cannot call him that to his face. Kokumo got his own name from his parents because he was an *abiku*, he had died and come back to life many times and so the name was given to him to prevent him from dying again. Now that he was soon going to become a teenager like me and was still alive, his parents were convinced that he wouldn't die anymore. That was why they were able to release him to go learn how to become a mechanic.

OUR BREAKTHROUGH CAME during one of the fuel scarcity periods. The last major one that lasted for over two months. It was not the money we were making every day that was even the breakthrough. It was the one we found in the boot of one of our customers' cars. It was Kokumo who found and took the black nylon bag while the customer watched Anywhere-belle-face and I to be sure we were pouring in the right amount of petrol in the fuel tank. The customer, a fat rich man with pot-belly, had asked us to fill one of the kegs in the boot and then put in his car as well. Kokumo filled the keg and dropped it in the boot while we filled the car. When the man paid us twenty thousand in total for fuel of six thousand on a normal day, we were so excited but couldn't show it. But then we didn't know what was waiting for us back at the uncompleted building where we usually met after we sold out our stock. Kokumo brought out the nylon bag and poured the money on the floor. I wondered how he had managed to hide the nylon bag without any of us noticing him and how he had even figured out what was in it. We couldn't be bothered. We wanted to go crazy, but we couldn't shout too much so that nobody else would hear us. *Walahi*, I have never seen that type of money in my life before. It is the type of money you see in the films they show in the once-a-month cinema, the type only the villain has and the hero has to kill all the bad people to get it back. We danced around the money like *ogbanjes* for about ten minutes, singing all the loud songs we could remember. We sang *Zombie oh zombie* and *Papa papa papayo...Send down the rain*, and many others. Then we carried Kokumo up like those footballers who win tournaments always carry their coaches up. His wisdom had delivered us from poverty. We had suddenly become richer than we could have ever imagined even without having to carry guns. God had seen the hard work and suffering we had endured all these years and had decided to reward us with abundance through his unmerited favour. That was what my mother said a week later, when I began to give her one note at a time everyday so that she would think I was making the money one by one like that, so that she would not see the big bundles and then think that her son had become a thief.

We shared the money equally, because that is what business partners do, so that no one felt cheated. But we gave Kokumo one bundle more even though he is the youngest; after all, he found the money and could have kept it all for himself. I knew my partners were not going to spend their money wisely, but I advised them to be wise like me and not start buying stupid things and then give people reasons to start suspecting us. I advised them to go and hide their money somewhere safe and go take from there whenever they needed it.

First of all, we were going to suspend all our businesses. With the money we now had, I was sure we could afford to buy a car, if not that we were too young to be seen driving a car around. We didn't need to work anymore, but to avoid suspicion, we would still wake up early, come out to meet somewhere, eat goat meat pepper soup and drink Tandi Guarana all day and go back home so that people would think we are still working and saving money. Then after about a month, we would give our parents part of the money and tell them to send us back to school. We would make sure it was the same government school so that we could all still be together. With our new money, we would wear new uniforms, not torn ones like other students. We would sew three uniforms from Kofi the tailor and also hire a maid who would be washing our white socks every day after school. We would be known as the three neatest students in the school and we would face our studies so that we could graduate in time and then go to the university. The university is the main place where we can enjoy our money. Maybe then I could finally find myself a girlfriend and start practising all the things I have been teaching Anywhere-belle-face. These were the plans I shared with my business partners before we left our kegs and gallons behind at the uncompleted building and walked away, never to return again. We headed straight for the fruit seller's shed just to teach him a lesson he would never forget. We bought his wheelbarrow load of fruits at once and paid him on the spot from Kokumo's extra bundle. Then we divided the fruits into baskets and took them home to our parents so that our families could finally enjoy what the rich people had been enjoying all these years.

That was how we truly became the breadwinners of our families.

EVERYTHING WAS STILL GOING ACCORDING TO PLAN a week after our breakthrough, after I began to give my mother one thousand naira every day and she would ask me to kneel and she would pray for me that there would continue to be fuel scarcity until I could save up enough to go back to school. But I began to worry when I started to notice that Anywhere-belle-face no longer wore his torn 'New York' t-shirt but had replaced it with t-shirts that had either 'Fubu' or 'Adidas' written across them. They always looked very expensive along with his new pair of jeans and shoes. Kokumo also no longer wore his black t-shirt and shorts, but he had gone to pay Kofi the tailor to make him flowing kaftans. I became very worried when I found out that Anywhere-belle-face also no longer did that thing with Kokumo's sister, but had instead chosen to patronise the loud whores at Kongi brothel every night. Kokumo had also gone back to Oga Deinde's workshop in his new fine clothes and shining wristwatch and given each of the senior apprentices who were lucky to be around when he came, one thousand naira each for beer. Those ones had told the story to the others when they returned and the news had begun to spread like a plague.

I tried my best to speak to the both of them quietly, like rich men, without shouting, that what they were doing was foolish. I reminded them that we had agreed not to draw attention to ourselves with lavish spending, but they said they only bought clothes and shoes and wrist-watches which people could have thought was from the prosperity of the lingering fuel crisis. I felt they had a point, until one morning, days later, when two policemen came knocking on my parents' door, holding

Anywhere-belle-face and Kokumo by their trousers. My mother came to wake me from sleep and in my drowsiness, I didn't understand what was going on until I looked across the road and saw the fat rich man with the pot-belly standing beside his car.

Pentecostal Sabina

That Sunday morning, I woke up early, at 5am, and did what I usually do on Sunday mornings. I went on my knees beside my bed to say a prayer. I woke up again thirty minutes later and realised I had slept off while praying so I got up from my bedside, went into the bathroom to wash my face and then returned to my room to pray, standing this time. After praying for about ten minutes, mostly inaudibly, and then reading two chapters from the book of Mark, I went back into the bathroom for a hurried bath and soon got dressed. I do not have breakfast on Sundays because I am a worker in church, and workers are expected to come fasting on Sundays. I have to get to church by 6:30am because I have to attend ushers' meeting, church workers' meeting, and then Sunday school before the main service. The main service was what ordinary members strolled in for from 9am, by which time I would already feel tired, yet it would be almost three hours of ushering later before I could eat. It is the work of the Lord.

When I arrived in church, the choristers were already having their dress rehearsal, which meant I was slightly late. I could hear Brother Kingsley, the choirmaster, taking the lead vocals.

Brother Kingsley and I are in a relationship, a courtship, but it is not the type of relationship you are familiar with. It is a holy relationship. Last October, when Brother

Kingsley realised that the Lord was leading him to me, he could not come to me directly to tell me that, because that is not the way things are done in the house of the Lord. He had to first tell Pastor's wife, who then called me aside after ushers' meeting the next Saturday to ask me if I was in a relationship. When I said no, she began to say that one of the most eligible young men in the congregation, who had been faithful in the service of the Lord, any young lady's dream of a godly husband, had come to her to ask if I was in a relationship. Then she said, Brother Kingsley, the choir master, was led by the Holy spirit to me and that she had told him to go and pray hard about it and get confirmation. She said the fact that I was not in a relationship was already a confirmation because God is not the author of confusion, but then she said I should pray about it.

Now, it is true that Brother Kingsley has a great voice, he is fairly good looking and God fearing, but the truth is that Brother Kingsley is not my idea of a husband. Besides, he doesn't look like he has much in his pocket let alone his bank account. That was a big concern for me. He doesn't even look like he has a well-paying job and I have never heard him give a testimony in church mentioning his job or office, or colleagues or anything like that. But I didn't tell her all these, I simply agreed to pray about it. Pastor's wife also hinted that wisdom was profitable to direct and that sometimes in life, there is a set time when certain things are destined to happen and that one needed to grab such opportunities in the lifetime of the opportunity. I nodded enthusiastically.

A week after I prayed about it, I went back to church to tell Pastor's wife that Brother Kingsley didn't really fit the image I had held in my mind of my dream husband. She laughed, the way she usually laughed when she cracked boring jokes during her occasional sermons and said I was being carnally minded, and to be carnally minded is death. She said Brother Kingsley may not look like much right now but that the bible says that he that finds a wife finds a good thing and obtains favour from the Lord. Besides, two are better than one and they have a good reward for their labour. Case in point, she said, was herself and Pastor. According to her, when she met him, he was a struggling itinerant preacher who knew he had a calling but had no money to pursue it. But the moment she agreed to spend the rest of her life with him, doors began to open. Look at what the Lord has done now, she offered.

Brother Kingsley didn't look like much to be honest, and I didn't see any correlation with Pastor. I couldn't tell if Brother Kingsley had a calling for music or simply had a gift and was using it to serve the Lord. Anyway, I told her that all was well and that I would consider it seriously, after all, I wasn't getting any younger, I told myself. And so, one week later, Brother Kingsley was given the green light to approach me and we began our courtship by registering for pre-marital counselling where we were given all the rules guiding a godly courtship acceptable unto the Lord.

No public display of affection until marriage. No petting, necking or kissing, even in private, let alone in public. The Brother and Sister shall address themselves as such, and not with pet names like 'Baby', 'Honey' or 'Sweetheart' until they are married. Under no circumstance should the Sister sleep over at the Brother's house, let alone live together, aka living in sin. The courtship shall be for a minimum of six months to afford the couple enough time to get to know each other. There shall be a pregnancy test two weeks before the wedding. If the Sister tests positive, there shall be no wedding.

The implication of the rules was simple; if you were not one of the pastors, you would not even know that Brother

Kingsley is my husband to be, because nothing we do or say suggests that. We don't even talk to each other in church anymore. Pastor says he will announce it to the church in two weeks, so that no other Brother or Sister would come to him saying they are led by the Spirit towards either of us. Then people will begin to come to us and say congratulations, and ask when the wedding would be and if they could be chief bridesmaid or groom's man or be part of the train. Nobody will offer to give us money to plan the wedding.

Even with all that, everything was going on smoothly between us, until about a month after, when I met Dennis and realised how tedious my relationship with Brother Kingsley was. It is not as if I am a carnal Sister, but Dennis reminds me a lot of my former boyfriends when I was in the world. He is the bubbly happy-go-lucky guy, the life of the party, the bloke every girl wants to hang out with. I was done with all that a long time ago. I am now a born-again Christian, washed by the precious blood of the lamb. I am one of those Sisters you see and you can immediately tell that I am born-again. I am not one of those new generation Christians who dress anyhow and claim the Lord only looks at the heart. It is not as if I am a Deeper Life sort, but there is something about my gait, my flat sole shoes, always flat, and my long skirts always reaching far below my knees that tells you that I am on the Lord's side. I am a classic spirit-filled, tongue-talking, demon-chasing believer, if ever there was one. Even my *christianese* vocabulary is testament to that, especially the 'it is well' and 'by the grace of God' - expressions I have learnt to use almost without thinking.

I never planned to fall in love with Dennis or anything like that. But then it is the spirit that is willing, the flesh is a weakling. The real problem, really, was just how different Dennis was from Brother Kingsley. How free, how lively and happy he was around me. You couldn't really say he was tall because we are of the same height even with my flat sole shoes, which meant that if I wore heels, I'd be looking down at him. But then he was quite handsome, in the way you would speak about an actor or a celebrity and he was fairly comfortable. Not rich, but comfortable. Car, house, good job, good shoes, latest gadgets and the like - basic checklist. There was only one problem. He wasn't born-again. He was a moralist. One of those guys who go to church at the beginning of the year, to cross over into the new year, and even then, take everything the pastor says with a pinch of salt. The type that look at you as if asking if you are really that gullible when you mention things like seed sowing, tithing and all.

It is easy to say what does it matter, especially when you are not in my shoes; when you don't attend a church like mine or have parents like mine who would not even hear of such. An unbeliever? Do not be unequally yoked. They know what they went through to finally get me to become born-again, despite growing up in a Christian family, so there was no way they were going to let me marry an unbeliever and make him the head of my home. But if the truth be told, I was already yoked with Dennis. At least in my heart. And remember Jesus said if it happens in your heart, it has already happened.

Dennis makes me happy. He makes me feel special in a way that no other man has ever made me feel. Right from the first day we met at the trade fair at the end of last year, when he introduced himself as Dennis Inyang and I told him my name was Sabina and we talked and talked while we went from stall to stall and then all the way to his car and throughout the journey home. It was as though we were long-lost friends who were seeing each other after a really long time, catching up. Weeks later, as we got to know each other better, I realised how much I enjoyed talking to him, mostly because I was free to express myself without restrictions. There was something I felt whenever I talked to Dennis that I had never felt for Brother Kingsley. My communication with my fiancé was so formal and I had to be careful about what I said or did not say, but Dennis was willing to talk about anything and everything - from the ingredients I was putting in the fried rice I was cooking to the colour of panties I had on at the moment. If there were any restrictions in our communication, I was the one who put them there. He was very direct. In a couple of weeks, he had already told me about his feelings for me and how he would love for us to be together. At this time, I had already said yes to Brother Kingsley's proposal and we had begun marriage counselling. Dennis was shattered when I told him this over the phone. He had grown cold and subsequently began to withdraw from me. I would have understood if he never got in touch with me again after that, but it was only for a few days. Soon, he resumed calling and texting me and asking if I would love to hang out with him sometime. Even if I wasn't betrothed to Brother Kingsley, there was no way I would have been allowed to marry Dennis anyway. So the best we could be was friends.

So, there I was when the service began, listening to the choir ministration led by my husband to be, and wishing it was Dennis singing. That he was born-again, serving the Lord in spirit and in truth in church with me and was preparing to marry me. I wished literally, that he could swap places with Brother Kingsley.

But it wasn't until the sermon began and Pastor began to talk about fornication and adultery being one of the reasons many Christians don't make much progress in life that the devil began to show me images of what it would be like to be in bed with Dennis. At least I wasn't a virgin and I couldn't marry him, so the least I could do was to have him, or let him have me, whichever, before I would finally marry Brother Kingsley and have to make do with whatever came with his package. The battle raged in my mind, right there in the service, while I ushered people into the few empty seats that were left at the back. Dennis sure looked and sounded like the kind of guy that knows what a woman wants in that department, not like the Brother Kingsleys of this world who may never have had more than one girlfriend before now and would therefore need a lot of help and tutelage to satisfy a woman in bed. I tried harder to get the ungodly thoughts and pictures out of my head and concentrate on Pastor's message and on keeping a few sleepy members awake to do same. But just when I felt I was beginning to succeed at that, I looked back briefly towards the church entrance, and there he was, coming through the church's open doors.

I thought I was probably fantasising, so I steadied my gaze and looked closer, but it really was Dennis Inyang, coming through the doors in a black suit and shiny black shoes with a black bible in hand to match, as the rising sun outside the church building hung just above his head. He looked like he had just stepped out of *Vogue* and was on a mission to derail a pentecostal sister and make her life a living hell.

Our Pastor is Hooked on Porn and Me

MY MOUTH HAS STAYED OPEN for several seconds now, and so have my legs. They are hanging on Pastor Ladi's shoulders and I don't seem to be able to move either of them because I am too shocked to see who just opened the door.

Everything seems to have run through my mind in this one minute, like a movie, one that must never be released. I had been Pastor Ladi's secretary for only three months when this rubbish began; after he singled me out of the church choir to become his secretary. He said he once had a dream in which God told him that I was the one chosen for this role and in it would I fulfil purpose.

The first time I saw pastor, on TV, I knew he was a true man of God - anointed and sent by God to deliver this generation from all oppression of the devil. Pastor Ladi is a fine man of God. That must be said. He is the kind of man you pray would at least keep you as a concubine, if he can't be your husband. And I'm not just referring to his amazing Italian suits and distinctive haircuts that you see on TV, or his bright white eyes that complement his shiny white teeth. His broad shoulders and steps that scream charisma. Not just that, I have seen what you have not seen.

"MUMMY IS A VEGETABLE IN BED!" he yelled. I had never heard him talk about his wife that way before.

I was sure it wasn't him speaking, it had to be the demons. I knew when it was Pastor Ladi talking, like when he quickly corrected himself and said, "Sorry, I mean, she is always so boring, so flat," and then the demons completed the sentence for him: "Sandy baby, you have to understand." His voice was pretentiously calm.

"Anytime I see you from behind when you leave my office, something happens in my brain."

"Sir?"

"I'm serious, Sandra!"

"But sir, you always say that Job made a covenant with his eyes..."

"Am I Job? Tell me Sandra, did Job marry my kind of wife?" The demons. They paused and an awkward silence followed. Then he broke it.

"Sandra, please, it will remain a secret between us. Nobody has to know about this. You are simply helping your pastor save his marriage; you are doing a good thing, please."

I couldn't believe my ears. Pastor Ladi? The same Pastor Ladi? This had to be the work of our adversary, the devil, mentioned in the book of First Peter Chapter five, no doubt about it.

Well, that was about six months ago now.

And yes, you can crucify me all you want for letting pastor have his way with me, but I doubt if you would have wished to be in my shoes for one day. I wore those shoes for two full months before pastor took them off forcefully, against my will.

But then, he was clearly a happy man these days. Not that he didn't seem happy before, because you could never tell from Pastor Ladi's baritone or his ever confident steps that he was enduring a boring sex life. This happiness was clearly different. He had become extremely bubbly and was always animated. Everybody could tell that something was different about pastor. I could see something else.

The anointing of God departed from him a long time ago. These days, the kind of miracles that happen in church are those minor healings of headaches and stomach pains, unlike those days that cancer disappeared and tumours melted like wax as soon as pastor got on the podium to speak. These days, he almost has to push people down when trying to transfer the anointing to them, unlike those days when he could throw it from as far as the altar. What is that thing they say about having to exert force when the knife is blunt? Or maybe it's all in my mind.

I can't explain the feeling that came upon me the day I saw Pastor Ladi cry, a few weeks after we began to make out. They were the type that accompanied sudden realisation of wrong and subsequent repentance; those tears. He told me how he didn't really want to be doing this with me, how he felt guilty each time he got home and had no interest whatsoever in making love to Mummy. Not that she cared anyway. I'm sure he must have also noticed that he now had to struggle to do certain things he could do so effortlessly before, because of the anointing. He sounded very repentant and I was already beginning to think about bracing myself. But he was soon back in-between my legs after only a couple of days. "I can't stop thinking about the last time," he said.

PASTOR ALWAYS SAYS THE RIGHT WORDS when we fornicate. He knows exactly what to do and say at the right time. If he is not asking you a question, he is producing those encouraging moans and groans that tell you you're doing something right. He knows when to touch and when to refrain from touching. I can't say more than this, I am a born again sister. This in itself was what made me begin to worry when I began to worry. I always wondered how come a pastor was so good in bed; how come he never needed help with anything when it came to lovemaking and he always assured me I was his source of joy and told me a million and two extra reasons why I must never leave him. Until today.

PASTOR CAME INTO THE OFFICE in a flurry and scurried back out almost immediately. He didn't even remember to compliment my new hair-do as usual. He simply told me to print out his flight schedule and then dashed out for the meeting he was to have with the HODs.

When I was ready to go into his office, I took the Don Moen CD I was playing along with me so I could continue playing it on his laptop as I worked. As I opened his CD-rom, something slid out. A DVD. I couldn't believe my eyes. He must have forgotten it in his laptop.

The perfectly shaped women whose pictures were on the disc, the shape of their breasts; I knew they were sham; it had to be bust enlargement or something more ridiculous. But these were the women mummy and I were meant to compete with in pastor's life. Mummy didn't even stand a chance here. My feet weakened steadily.

Then it hit me how much of a fool I had been. I was simply pastor's cheap way of fulfilling his sexual fantasies. Little wonder, I thought. This explained all the crazy styles and funny comments pastor made whenever he was behind me with me looking back at him, moaning. Like when he spanks me and asks, "Who's your daddy?!" and I'm thinking he is referring to the fact that we call him 'Daddy' and call his wife 'Mummy'.

I became overwhelmed with guilt. I wanted immediately to stop sleeping with pastor. After all, I'm not really his only source of joy - I am in fact, just a toy. But where do I start from? How do I tell anyone that our pastor, the highly revered Pastor Oladipupo Williams of Church Gate Sanctuary, is hooked on pornography and on me?

Well, I was going to talk to him when he returned from that meeting. I would tell him that I had discovered his secret and that I wanted out of this whole thing. I cried in the mean time.

PASTOR RETURNED VERY LATE. I had fallen asleep and woken up twice on the couch in his office by the time he did.

"Sandra!" He tapped my bum. He must have been calling me for a while as I stretched out of slumber. "Have you printed my flight schedule?" he queried, making his way to his table. His voice quaked, like he had been shouting.

"Yes sir," I said reluctantly.

"When do you want to go home today? It's getting late, and everybody else is gone," he began as usual. I knew what was to follow but I wasn't having any of that today.

"I'll leave after I have a word with you, sir." I had never really been able to throw the 'sir' away despite all our sexual escapades, but I dwelt on the word now so he could get the message.

"What's it about?"

I sat up on the couch and walked towards his table. I wasn't really sure how to go about this anymore. Do I turn this into a shouting match and in the end walk away telling him it was all over between us? Or do I just play along for a bit and see if he would deny or own up?

"What is it Sandra?" His fractured voice interrupted my thoughts. He was already coming towards me. He was that way, very caring and always very concerned.

"I want to ask you a question, sir."

He lifted me and placed me on the table gently and began to fondle my breasts.

"I want us to talk, please, sir."

"About what? I've missed you." I dodged as he tried to kiss me. It landed on my cheek and then he kissed me, moved down to my neck and nibbled. He knew I would lose control if he did this.

"Sir..." my voice began to quiver like his. His right hand was between my legs.

He lifted my blouse with his left and tried to pull it over my head and then I helped him. My blouse hadn't even landed on the floor when I felt his hands on my breasts, setting them free from my bra. He must have learnt this from the DVD too. I wanted to push him away, but my hands went around his neck and I pulled him close and kissed him.

He laid my back on the table and released his belt.

His trousers fell to his shoes, and then he lifted my legs and placed them on his shoulders.

That was when I heard the sound of the door opening.

The Lump in my Celibate Throat

FROM CHILDHOOD, I HAD ALWAYS DREAMED of becoming a pilot, to sit in the captain's cabin of a fully loaded passenger plane and lift it far above the ground, high into the skies. At other times, when I began to hear stories about how people hardly ever survived air disasters, I would think of becoming an engineer, or at those times when I watched TV and saw how doctors in the movies and soap operas were always treated with so much respect, I would think of becoming a doctor, if only fleetingly. At no time in all my childhood years did I ever think of becoming a priest of the Catholic Church, neither did I ever think of it as something one could even *become*.

I felt it when I woke up this morning, that lump I had first felt as a boy of about eleven or twelve, the day I woke up to sounds of an argument between my parents. I began to feel it when I heard my mother's loud voice yelling, "To the seminary he must go!" while my father's more placid voice was almost muffled, saying, "Let God decide, please," repeatedly. I knew his words were no use because my mother always had her way.

I did eventually go to the seminary, even though I didn't understand why I had to, neither did I fully realise the implications. But I soon understood much when I got there. God must have decided it from heaven, just like my mother would say to me later on, "because you are his workmanship, created unto good works which he had before ordained that you should work in." She would turn the pages of her old dog-eared bible and show me that in the tenth verse of the second chapter of the book of Ephesians, as she spoke.

If only I was her first or only child, maybe mother wouldn't have insisted on her son becoming a priest. But my elder sister's six month old condition gave my mother hope of a grand-child, and so on me, her son, hinged her other aspirations, of respect and honour. I had always observed the honour and worship and gifts that were regularly bestowed on Father Fidelis and his family, even though he had no nuclear one. Not many realise that it was the kind of respect which came at a great price.

IT'S BEEN WELL OVER TWENTY YEARS since that night now and I am still celibate. I have never known the feeling of being with a woman. Whenever the thought of the alluring pleasures of coitus begins to cross my mind, I pick up my rosary and make the sign of the cross three times, from my forehead to my chest and then across my shoulders. Such thoughts are of the devil who will always try hard to attack my conviction and chastity with evil thoughts. That was what we were taught at the seminary. If it persists, I would have to depart from solitude and seek the company of other children of God.

The closest I had ever come to knowing this pleasure was the day before that night of the lump in my throat. I had been out playing *hide and seek* with the other children in the yard. I had found Ngozi, the daughter of my mother's friend, hiding behind the make-shift toilet slightly shielded by banana trees, and she had placed her right index finger over her lips, gesturing to me not to declare that I had found her. She must have been about three years younger than I was. I don't remember where the idea came from, but I remember quietly demanding that she pull her skirt up so I could see her panties if she didn't want me to declare that I had found her. She had reluctantly but quietly obeyed. I don't remember removing her pants, but I remember putting my hands between her legs and just as I did, I felt myself growing hard. It was the sound of the footsteps of another child coming in our direction that made me remove my hand and drop her skirt. She began to avoid me from that day.

I HAVE TO GET OUT OF BED and do something before these thoughts begin to defile me. I swallow some saliva, pushing it deliberately past the lump in my throat. I pick up my bible and rosary from the stool beside my bed. As I get on my knees to pray, I hear the sound of the doorbell coming from the living room. I look up at the wall clock. It is 5:30am. I decide to wait a bit; maybe I hadn't heard anything. The sound returns after a few seconds, so I get up and walk briskly into the living room, past the dining table and chairs, to the front door. I draw the sign of the cross across my head and chest quickly. I look through the door hole and I am greeted by the frame of a woman, darkness still cloaking the morning. I hesitate a bit to think about what this person could be doing here so early. Is she in some form of danger? I hope not. I open the door.

"Good morning Father."

I recognise her. Sister Jennifer, one of my parishioners. She always wears different gaudy scarves and a smile. She isn't wearing any today. Her hair is full and flowing. Her eyes are bright even though it is morning, like she has had no sleep and has no intentions to do so. She has a wrapper woven around her body from her neck, as if to further shield herself from the cold.

I open the door wider and step out, shutting it behind me. It is really cold outside.

"How may I help you, Sister Jennifer?"

"It's a matter of life and death, Father. Please can I come in? I don't want people seeing me in front of your house so early."

I can hear my heart beating swiftly. I look around rapidly, and then I try to think as quickly as possible. Was someone dying? What could she be here for so early? Then her voice interrupts...

"Please Father."

She must have noticed my hesitation. I turn and open the door. I enter and stand by it as she walks in. She stands close to the entrance and requests for some water, barely audibly, but I am able to pick out her words in the stillness of the morning.

I ask her to take a seat as I walk smartly into the kitchen. I begin to say a prayer that whatever situation has brought Sister Jennifer to my door so early in the morning, the Lord will be merciful to resolve it. I open the fridge and bring out a bottle of water which I pour into a glass before returning to the living room.

I look at the dining table as I return to the living room, my eyes searching for a saucer on which to place the glass before presenting it to Sister Jennifer. Then I hear her voice.

"Father, I came to offer myself to you. Please take me."

The glass of water falls out of my hands as I turn to look at her, the glass meeting the concrete floor and dispersing its content and pieces in different directions. I stand still as shivers travel from my feet through my spine into the back of my head. I want to scream and I suddenly become thirsty, for that glass of water that has now become a shattered mess on the floor. Never has a woman offered her nakedness to me this way before. I think of praying the rosary but I do not speak. I think only of her rounded breasts, still so firm and pointed for someone her age, and her hips so broad and obliging.

Then she begins to walk towards me. I think of going to meet her right in the centre of the living room, to throw off my pyjamas and let my hands grab her breasts, soaking in their double tenderness. To loll into her embrace and experience the hidden pleasures of a grown woman's flesh. The thoughts suddenly become blurry in my mind and so does the image before me. In their place, flashes of scripture: *Lust not after her beauty in thine heart; neither let her take thee with her eyelids...For by means of a whorish woman a man is brought to a piece of bread: ... But whoso committeth adultery with a woman lacks understanding: he that doeth it destroys his own soul.* Impulsively, I begin to scream. I do not know why but I scream at the top of my voice and begin to walk backwards till my back is against the wall. I do not know exactly what I mouth but it must have contained 'the Blessed Virgin Mary,' 'Jesus Christ,' and any other thing that makes her suddenly stop walking towards me. It seems it frightens her, or maybe it is the thought of the neighbours hearing my voice and coming to my rescue that stops her in her stride.

I watch as she picks up her wrapper and covers herself just as she came. I try not to look at her but instead I keep my focus on the Blessed Virgin Mary, the frame hanging on the wall behind Sister Jennifer.

She turns her back sluggishly and begins to walk slowly out of the door. I want to stop her, to tell her not to leave. I want to see more, to know and experience what she wants to do to me, but I also do not want to be a partaker of her iniquity.

I sit slowly on the floor and swallow past the lump in my throat. It reminds me that she will be back. Soon.

Witch-hunting Nights

IF YOU ARE A CHILD, LIKE ME, and you live here in Enin, you should know that recent nights have not been the best. These days, nightfall for every child comes with a promise of doom and uncertainty, only brought to an end by the breaking of dawn, until the next nightfall. It is like war, foretold, yet from which you cannot run. You can only prepare; by doing your best not to look or act like a young witch or wizard.

They say there are several ways to identify a witch, or wizard. One night, I overheard Papa telling Mama the different signs of witchcraft in children. He had learnt them from the meeting of the household heads held at the village council hall. Prophetess Semanta had taught them, reading from a book. Papa told Mama so, but he did not say if it was a book with a title, the type we use in school as textbooks, or just a note the Prophetess had written by herself. I wish I could have the book, the one she read from, so I could know all about how not to be a witch.

The signs are very many, and so it is very difficult not to be a witch or wizard, eventually. Nearly all the things that playful children like to do are on the list of signs. This is why many children have been arrested, taken away and tortured. Some have died, which is why I decided to stop being playful. I read those signs again every time I hear that another child has been arrested because he or she was either found talking to an animal or placing his or her legs on the wall or looking at an elderly person with *evil eyes*. Especially if you have regular bad dreams and scream from your sleep, or while you sleep, you dream that you are in the toilet and then you release the content of your bladder onto the bed, you must be a witch. Every time I hear that another set of children, boys and girls, most of them my age mates, are facing the elders' panel, I silently thank God that I heard my parents discussing those signs and I had written them down, the ones I could write as Papa spoke in hushed tones that night amidst slow bites and careful chewing of his kolanut as he spoke. I had laid flat behind our long wooden bed where I couldn't have been seen, writing as Akpan and Mfon slept. Papa was on his armchair, facing Mama who was seated on the old stool, knitting with her needles.

Once caught, you must be prepared for all sorts of questions, like the name and location of your witchcraft coven, how you operate and who your leader is. You must also be able to tell the elders about your role as a witch or wizard - how many people you have killed or helped to kill, how many people you have cast evil spells on and how many people you wanted to bewitch but failed because Jehovah's power in their lives overshadowed yours, and they rubbed olive oil on their foreheads the night before and they had their bibles firmly under their pillows, so that the toothless elderly woman among them can shout 'Praaaaaaiiii the Looorrrrr!' and they can all say 'Halleluyahhh'. Failure to provide answers to any of these questions will lead to serious torture and if you are weak, death.

I MOSTLY FALL ASLEEP behind our long wooden bed. Half because I want to be as far away from the witch-hunters as possible when they come searching our house, and partly because it is tight on the bed with Akpan and Mfon, and I don't want to dream that I am being chased by the witch-hunters and then fall off the bed. That would immediately make me a witch and I'll be taken away. It will be said that I fell from the roof as I returned from a failed mission to eat someone up at night and suck their blood, or that the neighbours were praying like most households now do – *every witch flying in this community, fall down and die!* - while I was flying and so I lost my wings and crashed into our house through the roof. No one will ask why the roof wouldn't have a hole in it; after all, witches go through things.

I hear today is the last of the witch-hunting nights. I cannot wait for peace to return to Mkpat Enin after the end of this war against witches and wizards. The blame for this uprising belongs to no one else but Prophetess Semanta and her people, and their three days crusade which they tagged 'SUFFER NOT A WITCH TO LIVE'. I did not attend this crusade because Papa sent me to the farm. And it was a good thing Papa did that, although I did not want to attend because I didn't want to have anything to do with those people. If Jesus himself, the saviour, was to come to our community to hold a crusade, is this what he would call it? Papa later said to my hearing that he would have loved me to be there to see if the Prophetess would have pointed me out, so that he could be sure that he did not have any witch or wizard living with him. Thank God I was not there because I would have been a witch in her eyes because of the despiteful way I would have been looking at her.

It was during this crusade, as I heard, that the Prophetess began to point accusing fingers at children, calling them servants of Satan and asking them to be brought forward for deliverance by fire. She said it was these child witches (along with the elderly ones in the community who had initiated them to preserve witch-craft in Enin) that were responsible for the deaths and problems of the community. Once the elders heard that, they all let out exaggerated *Saaai* exclamations, lifted their hands and folded them across their chests while others placed theirs on their heads. I even heard that she accused the witches of not allowing rain to fall on our crops. The rainy season was over, yet the elders believed her and hired her after the crusade to begin these witch-hunting nights around the community.

TOMORROW IS CHRISTMAS, but there are no lights adorning our trees or sparkling lights at the main square. You cannot tell that a saviour is about to be born, because we all now live in fear; especially the little children whom the saviour said should come unto Him. I will sleep now, but just like most children, I will not sleep deeply. I will not snore and I will keep my eyes and ears open because that is the only way I now know to sleep. But still, I would not know when they would finally come, and what it is that I would do to make them believe I am a witch and take me away.

TERA WAS THE MOST QUIET one among us. She never spoke and she never answered any of the questions the witch-hunters asked her. "A stubborn witch." She must have been the youngest too. She had very small eyes and her hands were also very small. But I would later hear her scream the loudest when the youths come to tell us that her father had died and she was responsible. They, the torturers, would say she must have sent her spirit to the evil world to report her father to her colleagues for calling her a witch and her colleagues had come to kill her father. She would be tied up with her hands and suspended in the centre of the village council hall so that blood could flow to her head. And her small eyes would remain closed, her mouth refusing to let out any confessions.

As I looked into the faces of the other children, questions began to flood my mind. If all of us here were truly witches and wizards, do they not think that we would have used our evil powers to free ourselves? Would it be this easy to arrest and torture true witches and wizards? Like goats? They say the beating and torture is meant to drive out the spirit of witch-craft that is lurking in our bodies. They say that if the body, which is housing and accommodating the spirit, is made very uncomfortable, the spirit will be forced to leave. They make our bodies more uncomfortable by not giving us food or water for as long as it may take to get us to confess.

IN THE COMING DAYS when I would begin to feel lifeless, watching my spirit gradually leave my body day after day, more from starvation than the torture, I would see a girl, barely six years old take in a six-inch nail into her head and not die. They would say her witch-craft is strong and that she is one of those with nine lives. I would also see them use cold water to freeze out the spirit from the body of a boy after beating him thoroughly. This is usually the second stage if a person refuses to confess at the beating stage. This beating and freezing is meant to affect the spirit, the witch-craft, not the person.

There would also be a man, who would come to return a boy, his step-son, to the council hall, his hands and legs tied up like a sacrificial lamb. I would not be able to see clearly because by then my vision would have become very dim. He would dump the boy on the ground like a bag of rice he had been carrying with much perseverance and say to the leader of the witch-hunters, "Please deal with him very well. *The witch-craft never finish for im bodi*".

The Young Witch of Ifewara

JEMILA WOKE UP WITH A BAD TASTE in her mouth that morning. She would have loved to simply remain on the mat and not go to school, but there was one reason she had to be in school today.

Today was the teacher's judgment day, the one who had dared to flog her for being on the list of noisemakers. It was the first time her name was appearing on the list, and she knew that it was because Ife, the class captain, simply wanted to get back at her for defeating her at *suwe*, the game the girls played at break time, casting stones into squares drawn on the ground and hopping into them on one foot. She could forgive Ife for that, because she had indeed made a bit of noise in class that day. She knew she could always get at Ife if she wanted to, after all, Ife's younger sister was at her mercy now. But she could not forgive the teacher for not forgiving her since it was the first time her name was appearing on the list. She couldn't forgive the teacher for being so determined about her strokes and for inflicting that much pain on her. After all, everyone knew she never made noise in class. She could only sit on her right buttock because the left one still hurt slightly from the strokes even after an entire week had passed. And so she had told her friends that today, they should all come to school to witness the teacher's judgement. That was why she had to be in school.

She also had to be up to prepare food for her younger brother, Tantoluwa, dress him up and take him to his school before heading to her own Modakeke Primary School. Since her father left for the farm two days ago with her step-mother, Tantoluwa's mother, who Jemila preferred to call *Iya Tanto*, she had been enjoying the freedom she now had but it also came with a lot of responsibility. She didn't mind. It was the first time she was suddenly free to really do as she pleased and she was ready to do just that, although she still missed her step-mother in a rather impish way.

She brought her legs down from the wall and jumped off the mat. She released a loud yawn and spread her hands wide as she stretched. She bent and tapped Tantoluwa on his backside slightly, but he only adjusted his sleeping position, so she brought her right hand to her mouth, blew some air into it to add some more imaginary peppery feeling to it and then hit him with all the force in her hand.

"Yeeeeee," Tantoluwa screamed as he jumped out of bed as though he was being chased by a masquerade in his dream.

Jemila smiled an accomplished smile, and muttered something in Yoruba about her step-brother being the laziest seven year-old she had ever seen in this present life and the one to come. She asked him if he didn't know that work was the antidote to poverty and that anyone who intended to find good in life usually sets out early in the morning. Tantoluwa hissed and pronounced several childish curses on her in Yoruba, spreading his five fingers towards his half-sister.

THE TEACHER CAME TO SCHOOL with three members of her family - her husband, an aged uncle and her mother-in-law. Jemila had visited her in a nightmare giving her gory details of her proposed judgement which was to take place today. The teacher had woken up terrified, screaming and drawing the attention of her husband. It was he who advised that they go to the school to beg Jemila.

She had initiated two of the girls in her class who she felt needed help to stand up against boys who bullied them and teachers who victimised them: Rukayat, Ife's slim younger sister who was always crying, and Toyin, the daughter of one of the teachers. All she had to do was give them oranges. Black oranges. After their initiations at the meeting that night, she promised to take good care of them in school and ensure no one ever took advantage of them again as long as they remained loyal to her and followed her instructions carefully. She would give them certain incisions, *gbere,* for protection.

The *gbere* she made on Ruka's right hand was to make sure that any teacher who flogs her would experience a gradual swelling of the hand until he or she begs for mercy. It would also serve as protection against snake bites because Ruka usually went to farm with her parents. As for Toyin, after her incisions, she gave her a red rope to always tie around her thighs. Toyin was the kind of attractive girl some young men may want to take advantage of. The red rope was to ensure that any man who tries such with her would meet his untimely end even before he could have his way with her.

Jemila never spoke English. She didn't know how to. She spoke fluent dialectical Yoruba garnished with proverbs beyond her age. Even when teachers asked her questions in class, she answered in Yoruba. Her classmates knew better than to laugh. She dragged her feet whenever she walked, kept coins inside her budding breasts and also always scratched her body, but most of her classmates knew better than to 'look for her trouble' by engaging in any side comments about her. She had taught a few of them lessons they would not be able to forget in a hurry and the news of her capabilities had been spread effectively.

Once, a male classmate had tried to fondle her breasts on her way from the toilet. She had said nothing to him and simply wrestled her way out of the situation, but the boy soon returned to class and found out that he could no longer speak. She had made him dumb. This lasted for the rest of the day until the entire class got worried about the boy's inability to speak. After school, she walked up to him in the full glare of students who were making their way out of their classes, stood on her toes to be able to match his height, issued him a strong warning about his earlier action and followed it up with a loud slap. He began to talk.

Incidents like that were now common knowledge within the school which was probably why the teacher's mother-in-law didn't mind kneeling down before Jemila to beg her for forgiveness. Who would want a little girl to make her daughter-in-law barren or worse still carry a pregnancy for twenty-four months?

"E ma so oluwa re lenu o jere. O da na mo ti gbo." Jemila was embarrassed by the openness and unashamed approach the teacher had decided to employ in begging her. She had no choice than to forgive in order to avoid more harm to her already damaged reputation. She wondered what she would do with the padlock she had brought to use to lock up the teacher's fate, now that she had decided to forgive her. She had even thrown away the keys to the padlock on her way to school in order to put some finality to the judgement. These things were always useful anyway.

She couldn't wait for her parents to return from the farm, so she could narrate her recent conquests to her step-mother. It was her step-mother who initiated her into witch-craft after she got married to Jemila's father. Jemila was about six years old then. *Iya Tanto* had woken her up in the middle of one night and ordered her to swallow two black boiled eggs. *"Gbemi! Ma je o!"* Swallow, don't eat it, she had instructed, before a visibly frightened Jemila began to swallow painfully. Jemila's step-mother later told her that she had sacrificed all her three children from her previous marriage, and they had been feasted upon at different times by the twelve remaining witches in her coven. Tantoluwa was being spared because he was of a different father and she had also promised to initiate a new child every year, either directly or through one of her previous converts.

Jemila smiled a knowing smile as she walked home later with Tantoluwa, swinging her bag happily, in anticipation of her step-mother's return. As they approached their home, she spotted a car parked right in front of their small hut. She stood still for a while, not able to comprehend the sight. Cars like this were only seen in the big city. Who owned the car? One. Why did whoever the owner was have to park the car right in front of their house? Two. Was it to mock them? That they were poor and could never afford a car? Three justifiable reasons why Jemila was going to deal with the car and the owner, whoever it was.

She led her brother into the hut, brought out the padlock she had kept in her bag, and went back outside. She held the padlock open in her right hand and began to walk round the car, speaking incantations. She went round the car three times, spoke into the padlock and locked it. She then went to sit under the guava tree opposite the hut, still in her school uniform, humming and waiting to see who the unfortunate owner of the car would turn out to be.

Soon, a dark skinned young man and an equally dark-skinned lady stepped out of nowhere and were already by the car when Jemila noticed them. She must have gotten carried away. She had wanted to see exactly where they would come out from. She was sure her step-mother had power to do this, know where a person was coming from without asking. She would also grow into such terrains of power, surely. The couple looked happy. They must be a couple either getting ready to be married or newlyweds. She began to feel sorry for them as the young man put the key into the ignition and tried to start the engine of the car. The engine let out a loud hiss. He tried again and again and shook his head repeatedly and hissed along with the car.

Jemila had imagined that she would be laughing at this point, and enjoying the fact that the man was being punished for coming to show off his car in front of their hut. But instead, she felt sorry. She felt as though by doing this to the man and his bride, she would never be able to find a man like this who would own a big car and come to meet her parents in the village one day to ask for her hand in marriage. She got up to go look for the padlock.

When she came back outside with the padlock, the man and his lady were out of the car. They had opened the bonnet of the car and were already beginning to sweat. She wondered why no one else had come out to meet them, after all, hadn't they come to visit someone? Or maybe they didn't meet anyone wherever they were coming from. Jemila had to find a way to convince them to open the padlock if they ever wanted to move the car from that spot, without telling them why they had to. She now regretted throwing away the keys to the padlock.

"*E kaa san o,*" she greeted.

The lady looked in her direction. "*Kaa san.*"

"*Oko yi'n yonu,*" she asked, as if she didn't know they had trouble with the car.

"*Beeni.*" The lady responded. Jemila was glad that she at least understood Yoruba because the man looked like he simply couldn't be bothered, until he spoke.

"*Se a le ri* mechanic *l'adugbo yi?*" he asked.

"*Ko si* mechanic, *sugbon te ba le bami shi agadagodo yi, oko yin yi o sise.*"

The couple looked at themselves and began to laugh. Who was this girl? Asking them to help her open her padlock and then their car would work? Nothing could be more hilarious.

Jemila shook her head pitifully at them as they laughed. Just then Tantoluwa came out from the hut to watch. After they laughed to their heart's content, the lady turned to Jemila and collected the padlock.

"You know what honey, see if you can help her open it. She probably wants us to help her before she will go look for a mechanic for us."

The man collected the padlock and went to the boot of the car to bring out a wheel spanner and a small hammer. He put the padlock on the floor, put the spanner through it and hit it hard with the hammer. The lock flung open.

Jemila smiled to the lady.

"*Oya e sha na s'oko*," Jemila beckoned on them to start the car.

The man looked away a bit like he hadn't heard and then looked at the lady as if waiting for a confirmation. She was expressionless, probably also didn't know what to believe. He decided to take a chance. He put the key into the ignition one more time and turned. The engine hissed again and then suddenly came to life.

Aminu-Suya

AMINU-SUYA SELLS THE BEST SUYA. Not that I
have been eating roast meat from different places and
then decided that his own is the best, I just think that
his suya has to be the best for everybody to be buying it. People
say that if you eat Aminu-suya's suya once, you will continue to
eat it for the rest of your life.

I have only tasted it once; the first day I found the
courage to ask him to cut small for me. He had just arrived and
was still setting up the raw meat just before darkness covered
both of us. He looked at me piteously with a smile, as if
sympathising with me for what the aroma of his suya must have
been doing to me. I tore the piece of meat with my teeth and
with so much joy. I did not want it to finish but it eventually
finished.

I had to wash my hands properly that day with the
accumulated water in one of my empty pure water bags because
Aunty must not perceive the smell of suya around me or she will
beat hell fire out of me and say, "All. Liars. Shall. Perish. In. Hell.
Fire!" A stroke always accompanies each word and the last word
always brings the most painful stroke.

Aunty is my mother, but sometimes I wonder. I hear she
gave birth to me when she was very young. She is still very
young but she is also very wicked, as if I am the reason God
punished her with poverty, for sleeping with too many men.

I have not had another taste of Aminu-suya's suya since

then, but I have not forgotten the taste. Of course I begged him again the following day, but this time he did not give me and I still don't know why.

Aunty does not know how I always manage to sell out the two bags of pure water sachets she apportions to me to sell every evening. She thinks I'm in between queues of cars in evening traffic, shouting, "Puuure water!" like the other kids who also hawk in the evening. All I have to do is stay near Aminu-suya, because I know that every one of the numerous people who buy his suya will need water. If they think they will not need water, I will tell them that the pepper in aminu's suya will kill them if they don't drink water. They always laugh and then buy my water.

The only problem with this sense I use is that I always perceive so much of the suya without eating it. I cannot buy it because he does not sell cheap suya. His suya starts from one hundred naira and it is small, like the one he cut for me that first day. I cannot beg him again, because now I know he will not give me. Stealing it is not possible because my hands cannot even reach it where he places it, even if I try. Besides, Aminu gets really angry when people try to cheat him.

I eat my portion in my sleep. Aunty has beaten me out of sleep several times because she said I was chewing so hard, and "anything you eat in your dream is the devil's food," she always says. But me I know what I eat in my dreams; it is just suya.

AMINU HAS DIFFERENT TYPES OF CUSTOMERS, but he tries to treat everybody equally. He has plenty regular customers and he tries to remember their names. There are some who are passing our bus-stop for the first time, but the aroma of the suya makes them stop to buy. And then there are big men who park their cars by the road because of him, but he will not leave the customers flocking around him like bees to attend to any big man. The big man has to get down from his big car and struggle like everyone else. The only difference is that the big man can afford to pick a big piece of meat and throw it in front of Aminu-suya, to get his attention.

"Aminu-suya!" Your voice must be the loudest for him to answer you first. "How much, that one?" It is the big man talking.

"One-five!" Aminu would shout too because of the noise coming from the bus conductors and those people who play loud music at the bus-stop so that people can come and buy their lousy records. He would not look at the big man, but at the suya, turning it around as if to be sure he has not mentioned a wrong price.

Other people would continue to shout his name so he can cut two hundred naira or four hundred naira or one hundred naira suya for them. He does not answer those one hundred naira people on time but they are the ones that buy my pure water the most.

"*Haba!*" The Yoruba or Igbo big man will say with a fake Hausa accent, just to make Aminu think he can speak hausa. "One thousand naira, *da'Allah*."

"Pay one-two," Aminu is likely to say, lifting the suya with his left hand, ready to return it.

"*Oya cut am*", the big man would say. "No onions *abeg*." Big men don't eat onions with their suya, I don't know why.

I DIDN'T COME EARLY on the day that was to be Aminu-suya's last at his suya spot. But I was early enough to witness the beginning of the end of the lives of two grown men. People had not yet begun swarming around Aminu to buy his suya.

"Cut suya for me *jor*, *were*." Kabiru, one of the area boys at the bus stop was fond of threatening Aminu and collecting suya from him without paying. They always called him Scorpion.

"Scorpion, *I don dey telli yuu, one day I go killi yuu for hia*."

It was Aminu. The angry Aminu.

"*Iya e, oloshi!*" Scorpion replied, stretching his five fingers and palms wide open towards Aminu to accompany his affront.

"*Iya for yoruba, na mama. No curse my mama, Scorpion. I go killi yuu if you curse my mama.*" Aminu gesticulated his own warning with his long knife.

"*Oloshi, ki lo fe se? Wetin you go do? Iya'laya e!* Your great, great, great grandmother!" He picked up a piece of suya, tore part of it with his brownish teeth, turned around and began to walk away.

Aminu left his suya spot and went after him. He pulled Scorpion by his shirt and turned him around. He moved closer to Scorpion and forced his right hand into his stomach. When Aminu pulled out his knife from Scorpion's stomach, there were pieces of flesh and blood all over it. Scorpion's suya laden mouth stayed open as he collapsed. People began to scream.

One of the other area boys quickly rushed towards Scorpion. He lifted him briefly by his shoulders and then dropped him. "*O ti ku!*" he shouted, placing his two hands on his head, confirming Kabiru's death.

Immediately, two other area boys grabbed Aminu and disarmed him. They began to beat him as the other area boys began to run towards the scene. I had to go closer and then I stood on a big stone nearby to see what was going on.

Soon, Aminu's face became covered with blood and I could barely recognise him except for the yellow vest and black shorts he still had on. I could also hear some of the area boys saying Aminu should be killed. Suddenly, I saw *Eru-iku*, one of the leaders of the area boys, charging towards the crowd, carrying a keg in his hands. I put my two hands on my head.

He pushed through the people and then began to empty the content of the keg all over Aminu. The strong smell of petrol filled the air. People began to step back and then he kicked Aminu towards his suya spot. The fire met him on his way there.

I covered my face with my hands. Aminu began to scream. When I managed to separate two of my fingers to allow me see through vaguely, Aminu's fingers were beginning to curl, like a witch about to pounce on a victim. He was on the floor, with fire all over his body, screaming, *"Waayo Allah! Waayo Allah!"* from what everyone could tell was deep excruciating pain as the fire consumed his flesh, producing a repulsive odour. The whiff from his now burning suya also hung in the air.

After burning like that for a long time, he gradually became silent, and stiff, and very black.

It reminded me of what Aunty always says about hell fire, where she says all liars will perish in. This may be what it means to perish. I hoped in my heart that she wouldn't end up there too, because of the numerous men that always come looking for her and the different lies she tells me to tell each of them.

I looked down at the object that was Aminu-suya. He will never come here to sell suya to anyone again, so I have to look for another way to sell Aunty's two bags of pure water every night.

Our New Neighbour's Wife

THE FIRST TIME I SAW our new neighbour's wife was the day she came to ask my mother for matchsticks to light her stove.

'Matches?' my mother asked, with as much genuine surprise as I also expressed at the dining table, eating breakfast and occasionally turning my head towards the door to listen.

'Yes ma, matches, to light our stove. Or can I also get some kerosene?' she added, 'When my husband comes back, we will restock and I will return them.'

I almost laughed, but I made sure I didn't.

'No, you don't need to return anything, madam. Give me a few minutes.' She shut the door carefully to quell any hope our new neighbour's wife probably nursed of coming into our house. My mother was like that - very careful about letting strangers into our house. Even artisans who came to fix things in the house were never allowed in except it becomes extremely necessary.

My mother went into the kitchen and then called out to my sister, Nkechi. I knew it was to help transfer some kerosene from the fifty litre keg into a smaller container so she could give to our new neighbour's wife.

I thought my mother was always too nice, too generous, sometimes. She could give anyone anything, as long as she had it and she could find a genuine reason to give it out. Many times, she would ask us to gather clothes we no longer wore - shoes, bags and such - to give to less-privileged children. I have never met them, these "less-privileged" children, but almost every quarter, our used clothes disappear. But my mother always makes sure we get replacements. Better replacements. So I never complain whenever she says it is time to give out our clothes. And she always leads by example. She often gives out her own clothes, bags, shoes and jewellery to Madam Paulinus, her hairstylist who comes to the house on weekends, twice every month, to fix my mother's hair. At least once in four visits, she would leave our house with a bag full of clothes.

Nkechi didn't answer, so my mother called out again, louder, before Nkechi responded and then walked past me into the kitchen. I observed my sister as she walked sluggishly into the kitchen in her three quarter shorts and spaghetti top, revealing the top of her twelve-year-old breasts which I was sure were still forming. I couldn't wait to see my sister grow into a woman. I would add my own list of items to whatever it was that would be demanded from the man who would eventually marry her.

I quickly ate what was left of my breakfast, picked up my plate and walked into the kitchen to drop the plate. Nkechi had bent over to pour the kerosene on my mother's instructions. I was hoping she would ask me to give the items to our new neighbour's wife, so I could at least put a face to the name. But my mother didn't even notice that I was in the kitchen, because her back was turned to me as she searched the fridge for what I was sure was a cold drink, possibly soda water or bitter lemon. That is how my mother loves to start her Saturdays. I walked out of the kitchen and then decided to peep through the window to see the woman waiting behind the door. I changed my mind and decided to sit on one of the chairs in the living room, from where I could see the door, until Nkechi or my mother opened to give her the items.

'Thank you ma, thank you very much ma,' she said as I

stretched out my neck to see through the space between the door and my mother's body. She was bending her knees repeatedly as though she wanted to kneel but something invisible was hindering her. I noticed her bulging tummy.

'Please don't mention,' my mother said in her usual way when people said thank you to her. 'My regards to your husband when he returns.'

THE SECOND TIME I SAW our new neighbour's wife was the evening my mother sent me upstairs to our new neighbour's flat, to give them some food items. Rice, vegetable oil, salt, onions and smoked fish.

'How can a family not have had anything to eat all day?' my mother queried no one in particular as she handed the items to me one after another, beginning with the rice in a black polythene bag. I placed the bottle of vegetable oil, the onions, fish and cup of salt inside the rice.

It seemed our new neighbour's wife had been coming to visit my mother whenever Nkechi and I were not around, because these days my mother spoke of her with a wary familiarity and a deep sense of compassion.

'Do you know that her husband was once a big man?' she once said while Nkechi and I watched TV with her one afternoon. 'They had a house in Garki and at least three cars at any given time.'

'So what happened to them,' my sister asked with interest.

'Well, from what she told me, I think he fell out with the minister who gave him contracts regularly because he delayed the minister's kick-back on one occasion.'

Mother also said they had four children, and that our new neighbour's wife was actually pregnant with a fifth child. We all kept quiet after that, a strange silence, as though anyone who spoke after that was committing an abomination. I searched my sister's face, and I could tell that just like my mother, she was pondering the implications of having so many children in such difficult times.

OUR NEW NEIGHBOUR'S WIFE was feeding her youngest child from a feeding bottle when I got into their apartment, while another child cried beside her. The furniture, rug and accessories in their living room spoke of stale wealth, and a complementary inability of the occupants of the house to continue to keep things in pristine condition. Even the paleness of her breasts, largely visible from the top of her loose blouse echoed my thoughts. I looked up immediately she raised her head, hoping she hadn't noticed where my eyes had been.

'My mother said I should give you, ma,' I said, stretching the polythene forward.

'Oh, please thank mummy for me. Thank her very much, o? Tell her that I will come downstairs to say thank you once I finish feeding Elijah.'

I left their apartment in a hurry, even though I wanted to stay. I wanted to ask her questions, about their former life, about the new one and about her husband and children. I felt a bizarre need to be her friend, yet I also sensed a conflicting need to keep away from her. Maybe it was her pale eyes, her bony shoulders and slouching posture that made her look subdued and the way her words made you want to pity her. I didn't tell mother that our new neighbour's wife would be coming downstairs because I didn't want to extend the conversation about her.

THAT NIGHT, I HEARD A STRANGE NOISE from our new neighbour's apartment. I wondered if anyone else heard it. It was the voice of our new neighbour's wife, just a few minutes after I had heard loud thuds on the main gate at close to midnight. I was sure it was our new neighbour at the gate but I wasn't sure if the sounds that followed later, upstairs, were of our new neighbour's wife weeping or if she was merely performing her wifely duties in a rather wild way.

THE LAST TIME I SAW our new neighbour's wife, was three weeks ago. She was in her casket, at her funeral.

Our new neighbour was there too. He wore dark sunglasses and frowned a lot. The other men and women cried. My mother also cried and I wondered why. I wanted to cry too, so as not to look out of place, but I couldn't stop thinking about the noise I heard that night. I kept looking at our new neighbour's face as though something in his face would tell me exactly how his wife died; but it said nothing, just a frank, stable glare.

I tried to remember how he came rushing downstairs and banging on our front door early that morning to ask for help, saying his wife was bleeding. I remembered how my mother had rushed in and out with her car keys and ordered me to go call the landlord and open the gate. The landlord didn't answer, so my mother and our new neighbour had carried his wife into my mother's car while I opened the gate for them. Our new neighbour's wife was still alive then. My mother said she stopped breathing when they got to the hospital. She said she was confused because if it was just an unfortunate miscarriage, it really shouldn't have led to death.

I NEVER SAW OUR NEW NEIGHBOUR AGAIN after the funeral, till he moved out of our house with their four children. I had returned to the boarding house the day they moved. My mother still talks about them. How they now live in Garki, in a house not far from the one they had once lived in, during their first stint with wealth. How our new neighbour now drives a black Toyota Land Cruiser SUV and how they now shop at expensive places in Maitama. But my mother never mentioned anything about another woman. I heard that from Nkechi. She said that she also heard that he originally hired the woman to take care of his four children, but that her own tummy too was now beginning to bulge, because they say it is the heads of children that call forth more children.

The Sex Life of a Lagos Mad Woman

U
NCLE STARTED COMING INTO MY ROOM one week after I moved into his house. It was in March, about seven happy-new-years ago now. I am not sure about that figure, but I remember that it was the year my parents died. He really caught me off guard that first time. I was already sleeping when I heard the sound of the door opening and saw him tip-toeing into the room with his big pot-belly. I jumped up on the bed as he turned around to turn the key in the lock before switching on the lights. I was naked, the way I really loved to sleep in those days, and so I quickly grabbed my bed sheet and tried to wrap it around myself.

'Why are you afraid?' he asked, smiling. 'I just came to see how you are doing.'

I looked straight at him. His belly was his most distinctive feature without a shirt on. He was extremely hairy above the belly and he wore white shorts which seemed to intercept the hair that flowed down to his legs from his chest. I could see a slight bulge in his shorts which told me this wasn't a how-you-are-doing visit, but I gave him the benefit of the doubt. Seeing my nakedness might have caused that, I thought. I still used to give a lot of benefits of the doubt in those days.

'Sir...why did you lock the door, sir...' I stuttered.
'Oh that? Is that why you are afraid?' He turned around to turn the key behind the door, setting the locks free.

I quickly moved to my wardrobe to put on something. I turned my back to Uncle, covering myself with my bed sheet and trying to put on my pants. That was when he grabbed me. The ease with which he lifted me was frightening, considering the image I had seen of him moments before. My bed sheet and pants were on the floor by the time he dropped me on the bed. I began to struggle. I struggled and screamed even though I knew there was no one else in the house that could hear me. His weight on me was like trying to wriggle free under the weight of two bags of rice. He smelled like overripe plantain.

He eventually had his way, and I cried bitterly after. He didn't see me cry because he fell asleep almost immediately after he came. Uncle was a very lazy man in that area. In fact, he was already snoring; probably exhausted from the struggle I made him go through before the act.

That is when I could have killed him if I wanted to. I could have gone straight to the kitchen, picked a knife and cut off his thing. But I did not. I was too timid to do things like that then. What would I say happened to him? How would I dispose of his bulky body? If I decided to run away after that, where would I run to? Those were the things I kept thinking about. So I just cried, not because I wasn't used to a man's thing, but because no man had ever caught me off guard, taking advantage of me like that. Every time I had been with a man before then, it was because I really liked the man and wanted to give myself, freely. It was like that with Timi and all my other lovers after him.

Timi was my first love, and the first man to get in between my legs. It was a reward for waiting through our secondary school until we both got into the same University. I decided to let him have me in our second year. He was reluctant initially because he believed sex would make our relationship cheap, that we would become too familiar and we would no longer value each other. I wonder where he got all that from.

But I should have listened to him. I don't know if it was the regular sex we were having that caused it, but we became just as he had predicted - too familiar with each other and no longer valued each other. Sex became the only thing we looked forward to, unlike the days after we finished from secondary school, when we looked forward to going to the beach together and talking for long hours under the sun without the thought of even getting under each other's clothes.

I wonder if young boys still come in the mould of Timi. His father had been a Pastor and he was clearly well brought up. He bought me my first Bible - a Students' Study Bible - as my gift for passing my Universities Matriculation at first sitting, just like him, and tried to get me to read it often without much success. After we got into university, I kept looking forward to the day when Timi would ask to sleep with me, but he never did. By then, I was already extremely curious about sex. Maybe because of all the romance novels I had read and the movies I had seen. I wanted to know what it felt like to have a man between my legs even though I already knew how it felt to have my own fingers there.

So, one afternoon, in our second year, Timi came to the hostel with me during lectures because he was free and I had missed a class for getting there late and the lecturer didn't let me in. My roommates were all in class and so I decided to give Timi his long awaited gift. I'm not sure he valued it as much as I valued giving it to him, because he didn't look too happy afterwards. Maybe because he didn't see any blood. I had not been with any man before him, but I had broken my hymen myself mistakenly in secondary school when I began to touch myself and fondle my breasts to derive sexual pleasure. Maybe that was why things got stale too quickly with Timi. He had always talked about marrying a virgin, which was why he was also keeping himself. But maybe he no longer saw me as a virgin after that, or he didn't think I was even one before I gave myself to him. We never talked about it. It is the part of our story I still do not understand, even after all these years.

I watched Uncle sleep and snore, his belly rising and falling like a balloon that was being pumped and deflated. I no longer felt like killing him. I began to wonder why he was so small down there, and why I had felt almost nothing from his thrusts. It seemed thoughts of Timi had taken my mind off Uncle's earlier act. I just watched him sleep and then got up to wash myself in the bathroom.

***

UNCLE BEGAN TO BUY me gifts after that. Plenty gifts. Clothes, shoes, bags, necklaces, panties and brassieres. He even bought me a mobile phone with which he said I could speak to him whenever he was not at home and I needed anything and then he said he was going to set up a supermarket for me in Lagos. I stopped struggling with him after that. Although the bras he bought for me were not exactly my size, I liked them all the same and I liked that he could even be that close to figuring out my bra size without asking me. There was this particular one he liked to see on me whenever he came into my room – the one with the matching panties. I liked it too, because it made it easy for him to enter into me. I didn't need to take the panties off, I just pulled a rope in front of it and it created space big enough to take Uncle's small manhood.

The gifts were what made me begin to enjoy being with Uncle. And then there was the affection he showered on me whenever he was at home. I had never known such affection before then. I had never known that I could have such power over a man. No matter where Uncle was and what he was doing, I only needed to speak to him in a certain way over the phone, tell him how my body longed for him and he would leave whatever he was doing and whoever he was with and come home to me. Yet he would not come empty-handed. He would stop by at a boutique or gift store to buy me a gift on his way home. He stopped buying me food from those eateries because their food made me purge. I always cooked our food and he thoroughly enjoyed my cooking. That was another thing. He told me several times that his wife did not know how to cook like me, and she also did not spread her legs well for him.

'Those are the two things that keep a woman in her husband's house,' he said often. 'She doesn't have any of those two.'

I wondered if it was not the size of Uncle's manhood that led his wife to cheat on him with their driver, according to the story I heard, of how he subsequently sent her packing, after having the driver arrested.

For me, Uncle was all I had. He was the reason I still had a roof over my head and the hope that I would one day live a better life. He was the reason I had completed my education after the loss of my parents. So, being with him was the only way I could pay him back for all he did for me and the supermarket he was going to open for me. After all, what more did I have to offer him.

***

I REALLY DON'T KNOW how or why people began to call me Reveren' Sista, but I think it has something to do with the first outfit I wore for a long time when I first got here before I began to wear my crazy jeans. I found that first outfit, just like my new jeans, in the refuse dump. I'm sure it is that outfit, black and flowing to my legs, and then the cap that I found wrapped in one of them. It covered my head and still flowed down to my neck. I wore it for a very long time because I liked it very much. It covered every part of my body from the cold here.

This is my new home. It is not the type of place you want to call your home, but it is where I have lived since Uncle died. That should be about five years ago now, or six, or seven. I am not very good with remembering dates and years. His death took everyone by surprise, especially me. I ended up here after a few days, after his wife returned with his family members, and so many people I had not seen or known before then, asking me to explain how he died. I told them that Uncle slept and did not wake up in the morning, but they did not believe me. Especially his wife. She said I killed him. She said I wanted to inherit his wealth. She said she had heard stories of how I was fucking her husband. That was how she said it, in Pidgin English, the type that makes one wonder how come Uncle had married her. She went on and on about how she would deal with me. She was going to start by making sure I swore an oath in a shrine to prove my innocence. She wasn't going to let one small girl come and kill her husband and go scot free. She stressed my-hussss-baaaaand anytime she said it, as if she was really proud of him, as if she had not cheated on him first with their driver because of his small manhood and his inability to plant a seed inside her, before he found out and sent her packing. She didn't even beg to stay. As I heard, she abandoned him and went off. She is even rumoured to be going around with a younger lover these days.

It made me wish I had become pregnant for him, because of all the injustice he suffered in her hands. But I never did, not to speak of having a miscarriage. I wondered about it myself, but I never bothered about that because I wasn't even thinking of getting pregnant for him. It also never crossed my mind that he could die. If it did, maybe I would have considered that and made effort for him to get me pregnant. Now I had lost everything, even though in truth, I never really had anything.

'You must swear o, you must! Witch!' she kept shouting and raining insults on me as I sat helplessly on the rug in the centre of Uncle's private living room.

'Don't call her a witch yet. At least she did not say she will not swear. Let us be sure before we start accusing the innocent girl.' It was Uncle's elder sister. She was the only one who wore a white outfit, a blouse, wrapper and head tie, unlike the black outfits the rest of them wore, to signify that they were mourning. She was also the only one who seemed to have a white heart.

Everyone else in that living room that day agreed that I had to take an oath to prove my innocence, after which they would let me go in peace if I was found so. Since I knew I did not kill Uncle, I agreed to take whatever oath I had to take, to at least show the whole world that I didn't kill him.

Maybe the fact that I wasn't crying and screaming made some of them believe I must have killed him. I wasn't crying and screaming because for whatever reason, I was not sad that Uncle had died. I only became sad when I had to start living here, under this bridge, as a result of that. I was really indifferent about it all, strangely, even though I knew that would mean a radical change of life for me. How radical that change was going to be, I had no idea. I think my reaction had something to do with my temperament, or is it personality type they call it. I had read about it in a book Uncle gave me with clothes from a boutique he frequented. I knew because it was always the same polythene bag with *Women's Worth* on it. I can't remember the name of the book now.

***

A LOT OF THINGS CHANGED after that day at the shrine. My thoughts, my words, even the way I think and the way I talk, changed. My whole life changed. It was as if two wires joined together in my head to make it function well, were disconnected that day. Not that my head began to malfunction, but it began to appear to everybody from that day, that my head was malfunctioning. That's why they now call me mad. People now point at me and shake their heads at me. I am not mad, I am just not normal. But one day, I will be normal and it will become clear to everybody that I am not mad.

One of the things that also changed is that I no longer seem to be able to perceive odour like everybody else. From the time I moved here, I have noticed that people cover their noses whenever they pass this place. It means that something smells to them, that is why they cover their noses. That is what covering of nose is for, to protect you from smelly places and stinking things. But me and the grown men who smoke Indian hemp every morning, every afternoon and every night in that corner over there, always wonder what is making them cover their noses.

Another thing that changed is that I now like *faka fiki* a lot. Let me say, I like pounding, so that you can understand what I am saying. Not pounding yam. I like to be pounded often by a strong man with a strong something. Me that I could stay all by myself for months without a man, it is now impossible to stay for three days without desiring a man. Somebody must have put a spell on me. It had to be that bitter concoction I drank that terrible day at the shrine. At least I am grateful to the creator that I quickly got a boyfriend when I came here. I will tell you about him. They say the cow that does not have a tail, it is the creator that helps it drive away flies. It is not the creator that drives away my own flies; it is a man, a man with a big strong thing that I like so much.

He is the only man that knows that I am not really mad. He is tall, dark and very handsome. But I only wish he will learn to comb his hair and brush his teeth. But he is very shameless. His hair and beards are dreadlocked like my pubic hair, because he never combs them. His name is Rosco. He drives a commercial *danfo* bus and smokes a lot of Indian hemp. A lot. I fear it will destroy his brain one day. He calls it fish, *eja*, in his language. I don't know why he calls it that. Maybe so that people will not know what he is talking about when he sends one of those up and coming touts here to go and buy him two wraps of fish. But then, the way the boy will smile and smirk awkwardly, anybody in their right senses should know that it cannot be ordinary fish, because ordinary fish cannot make somebody smile like that.

Rosco shakes his head at me during the day, just like all the others in his gang and everybody else that passes by, but both of us know something they don't know. Both of us know that I am not mad, because at night, very late in the night, when all the others have gone, he will call me into his *danfo* bus, and I will do to him what that stupid *igbo* he smokes cannot do to him. But he is still my love, because, let me not lie, Rosco is very good. He is a man. The kind of man a woman can be proud of. He knows how to make a woman feel like a woman.

I wonder how Rosco even became my man. I think it was a divine orchestration to deliver me from the shackles of loneliness. Okay, I remember. It was in the night. One night, very many days after the last happy-new-year we shouted. I think it was the *igbo* Rosco smoked that night, along with the absence of those foolish *ashawo* girls, that made him notice me. Or maybe he saw my bare buttock when I bent down to arrange my things and prepare to sleep. Suddenly he began to look at me and smile and then he opened the door of his *danfo* and used his hand to call me to come. I thought I wasn't seeing clearly until I looked down at his trousers, between his legs. I left what I was doing and ran to meet him. I didn't even care if anybody could see us, even though it was very dark. That night was unforgettable.

I do not let him know I look forward to his thing every day now. How can I? Then he will stop squeezing that N100 note into my left hand every time he gets up after he has pounded me to his heart's content. He must think he has just raped a helpless mad woman as I watch him hide his thing and zip his pants. Fool. He does not have any idea how my legs shake uncontrollably and how I tremble in ecstasy and how the hair on my body stands when he is inside me. Only that he is always too quick. I don't know why, but I can't complain. Sometimes I want to grab him by his buttocks and make him stay there; but then he will know my secret. I have to wait till the next day or the next.

I'll continue to let him believe he is raping me but deep inside me I know I will die if he does not call me like that for three days. Especially on those nights it gets so cold here and you know that only a trip into sensual bliss can provide some respite, however brief. I don't ever want to return to those days of touching myself. How can I even think about it? Evil thoughts go back to your sender, please.

This place is always very cold, because there are no doors, no windows, nothing. But there is a roof. That's where the cars pass; plenty during the day and very few at night. The other ones who don't pass my roof usually pass my frontage and I love watching them, especially those ones that are as big as houses and you can't see the people inside because the glass is always black like charcoal.

***

TODAY, I WOKE UP DREAMING ABOUT TIMI. I still think about him sometimes, but it is difficult to think about another man, when you are with somebody like Rosco. Anyway, in my dream, it was my wedding day. I was getting married to Rosco and Timi was his best man. Then during the ceremony, when the pastor asked if anybody had any reason why we should not be joined together, Timi raised up his hand and began to confess that we were once lovers and that we were still fucking each other. Rosco got annoyed and began to strangle Timi right there in front of the pastor and congregation, and then Rosco disappeared and then I woke up. The foolishness of dreams.

I see a lot of strange things like that here every day

though. A lot of things. I will tell you some and then one that happened today. The one that made me swear that I am not mad and I can never be because I couldn't have done what the woman did.

Let me return to what I was saying before....the things I see here every day.

In the morning, I wake up with noise. Loud noise.

'Ojuelegba – stadium - barracks!' repeated four times in quick succession; if you don't live here you will think it is a call to war. I wonder where that is; a place whose name sounds like sport and war. Other times it is, "Itire - lawanson" that I can hear louder.

Where do I even know? I've not left this place for many happy-new-years now. This is where I shout it every time it is time to shout it. The death of my uncle is responsible for this. In those days, we used to shout it in church together, along with so many other people who you never see in church before that day. Some of them even come straight from beer parlours and brothels into the church when it is an hour or so to Happy New Year. They don't want New Year to meet them on top of a woman. Even my uncle, that was the only time he went to church in the whole year. The rest of the year, he would be busy running after money.

It is very early in the morning like this that Rosco wakes up and starts the engine of his bus. He will switch it off again and then go across the road and come back with water in a bucket. My eyes always go with him because I don't want any careless early morning driver to knock him down. When he gets back to the *danfo*, he will go close to one of the tyres and bring out that his big thing to urinate. That is when I always wish he would call me, but no, the fool will never even speak to me even if he sees me, he will most likely just shake his head like the others do when they look at me. I always have to wait till it's very dark.

Then he will remove his clothes and leave his shorts on, pouring water on himself with either a bowl or his hands. When it is time to chafe just below his waist, he will keep his hands in there for too long. This is why I know Rosco is a fool. Can't he just remove the shorts and wash properly? Who else is watching?

When he finally leaves with his noisy *danfo*, I'll turn my attention to the road. If I try to look out in the direction of the noise of sport and war, I will be able to see a man, or sometimes, a boy, hanging on to the door of one of the commercial buses. I will also see people; the so called sane people - male, female and school children, dressed either for work or school, rushing into the buses as though something is after them and they would only be safe in those buses. I am tired of seeing them, so I don't look at them anymore. Instead, I look out for the big black cars that look like houses; they always make me happy. If I feel hungry, I will get up, re-arrange my house and make sure no one stole anything while I was asleep, especially the last money Rosco squeezed into my hands, and then I'll walk across the road to buy what I'll eat.

Oh how I miss the woman who sells that early morning *akara*. She doesn't come again these days because of Governor Fashola's people. They said she needs to rent a proper shop to sell ordinary *akara*. So the woman decided to go and sell her delicious *akara* in her village, where they know the value of early morning *akara*. But I have found something better. I always go to the *aboki* who prepares tea and indomie noodles with egg. Only Rosco's thing is sweeter than that Indomie and egg in this life, you have to believe me. But the foolish *aboki* will not use his plate to serve me like other people, so I have to always remember to bring my own plate. He says I'm mad, yet, he knows how to collect my money and give me change. He doesn't toy with my change any more since the day he saw me bite a man with these my teeth for calling me "Reveren' sista". I hate that name. Those are the people who never do the thing me and Rosco do. They must really think I am one of such people. Fools.

I don't eat my food there, I always carry it back to my house to eat in peace because the so called commonsensical people never mind their business. They will be eating and looking at you with the corner of their eyes like a plague about to burst out of a pipe. As if that is not enough, they will now be shaking their head and muttering things to themselves like mad people. That is why I bit that man the other day after I heard him call me that foolish name. He didn't see it coming.

***

IT MAY BE BETTER TO ASK ME what I have not seen here than to ask me to start telling you the things that I see every day. I have seen rich men carry prostitutes away at night; I have seen a corpse dropped from one of those charcoal cars one night long time ago. I have also witnessed many fights between different gangs like Rosco's group where they use machetes on one another and leave blood everywhere. I have also seen many *okada* people die like chicken from too much speed, especially at that junction over there. Only last week, a speeding trailer climbed one *okada* rider's head spilling its contents to the ground. I couldn't eat for days after that. Let us not talk about it, please.

Yes, I promised to tell you about the incident that made me know that I am not mad, right? Actually that day I was just sitting on my own and I noticed a woman selling *Coke* and *Pepsi* and *LaCasera* and all these *jedi-jedi* drinks people buy and drink and then shine their teeth gleefully after only a gulp.

Suddenly she brought down the big container of drinks from her head by herself as if to sell to someone. Then she began to go round the container. Then she began to dance. Then I stood up. I wanted to understand what was happening. Then she started singing, and clapping like the people in those white garment churches.

Then she untied her wrapper and used it to cover her wares. That's when other people began to notice what I had been watching since. Then she removed her *buba*, revealing sumptuous breasts that made me jealous, only protected by a very fine bra with some *shine-shine* on it.

'*O ti n ya were o!*' a bus conductor yelled as his bus passed and people stretched their necks to catch a glimpse, saying the woman was experiencing the beginning of madness.

Then the men who were walking began to stop and look. I'm sure they were waiting for her to remove the bra. I took my eyes away.

I can't worry about her too much, because I myself I have a problem growing in my stomach. I feel like vomiting, and I am very dizzy and I am very worried.

***

I BECAME MORE WORRIED when I woke up this morning. I have been trying to remember what happened last night - if I saw Rosco and if anything happened between us. But I can't remember him calling me into the *danfo*, and I don't even remember seeing him this morning having his bath or leaving with his bus but his bus is not here. I must have over-slept. It is one of my symptoms, or am I also forgetting things?

I became more worried when I didn't see Rosco for two nights. It was now almost three days and I was sure I was going to die. He had never been away from here for more than one night. I have been through a lot in this my young life, I will not allow Rosco put me in this kind of situation and run away.

Later, I saw the rest of Rosco's gang wearing lace made from the same material, as if going for a ceremony, but I still didn't see Rosco among them, and it has been almost seven or eight days now. I have started vomiting and spitting and feeling very lazy.

Did someone tell Rosco that I am pregnant for him? Maybe the walls have heard it with their ears and told him and now he is trying to run away from his responsibility. Who wants to be the Father of a mad woman's child anyway? Or is Rosco getting married? But Rosco does not have a house. He cannot marry a wife into a bus, can he? And I have never seen another woman with him, except when he occasionally teases Radeke, the slim girl he calls *Lepa Shandy* - the one who sells Chelsea dry gin to him and his gang. Or maybe he was arrested and he is in the police station.

I tried to pay more attention to the conversation going on among his gang; maybe they would discuss something about him, but nobody mentions his name.

Then one evil thought came to my mind. Maybe Rosco has died. No. Rosco cannot die. He cannot leave me and go like that. Uncle can not leave me after he had been climbing me and then now, Rosco too? I was still thinking when I saw a big poster on one of the buses, it had Rosco's picture on it and EIGHT DAYS FIDAU PRAYER written above his face.

That was when I became mad.

I ran to the bus, shouting, screaming. I tore off the poster and began to roll on the ground. One of the men tried to get a hold of me but I did not stop rolling and I did not stop screaming. I got up and began to run. I took off my clothes and ran because now Rosco was gone, and my only hope of ever seeing him again was still inside me, and I would have to wait for nine months for *Babatunde*; for the father to come back again.

The Merchant's Dungeon

MERCHANT WAS NOT IN A GOOD MOOD today. I could tell from the way he was clutching his right fist and holding it in his left palm as if waiting to punch someone. He has been like this all day. It seems it is because of low patronage today. Or because of the young lady that died this morning in the cage, the one with the big breasts that Merchant had said was a big catch, "a whale" he had called her. We had woken up to hear screaming and wailing from the others in the cage, and Merchant had come out of his room to tell Gimbu to go see what the problem was. When he returned to say that one of the fishes in the aquarium had died, we rushed to the cage, and there she was, the whale, lying lifeless in front of the cage. Gimbu had dragged her out. Her short skirt had rolled further up to her waist, exposing her thin red panties while her breasts were out of her tiny blouse, almost completely, exposing nipples that were as dark as the inside of her thighs. Merchant kept staring at her body. I knew he was thinking, and I knew why he was thinking what he was thinking. So when he turned to me and said, "Cut up. For storage," I only wondered why Merchant always leaves out some words when he speaks, as if he expects you to still understand without them.

Although this has never happened before, a fish dying while still in the aquarium, it still felt like I had done this before – cutting up parts of a corpse neither I nor Gimbu had killed, for storage in the deep freezer, to prevent waste. It would no longer be sold as fresh parts, which meant less value, but at least it would still bring in money, sizeable money. I tried to do a quick calculation as I put the machete first through her left arm, and then her right as Gimbu held it out for me on the slaughter slab. Seven hundred and fifty grand for the head. I would cut it off next, after the limbs. All the limbs together, maybe three hundred. Her breasts would be the real deal, because of their size, along with everything beneath it – kidney, liver, heart, all priceless. We don't get breasts this big in every consignment. "Maybe because this was straight from the corner of one of the brothels in the city," Gimbu said. Maybe close to a million - the two breasts together, especially if it is a politician who wants to win an election. They don't negotiate too much. But it would have cost nothing less than a million flat if it was point and kill, straight from the aquarium. This is why Merchant is angry.

"We must never let happen. Again. This last time," he said later, as if it had happened before, or we determined who died and who lived.

Although, here, we do. Anyone brought in here becomes Merchant's property and he alone determines whether you live or die. No, you would surely die, at least when a customer comes asking for something that fits the description of a part of your body. But Merchant determines how long you live until then, except you are extremely lucky, like me.

I was once a fish in the aquarium too, seeing others dragged out of the cage for the slaughter slab as they screamed and cried and begged and held on to the others in the cage, others who were also waiting for their own day to come. One day, after Gimbu had dragged out a man from the cage and I had heard the man scream and groan in agony from the slab before Gimbu's machete cut through him, Merchant returned to the cage.

"Hey. You. Young man," Merchant said, pointing to me.

Merchant never shouts like Gimbu. He speaks gently, all the time, as if he needs space between his words to think of the next word, even when he is negotiating with our most difficult customers - the ritualists. I looked back in the cage. "You. Looking back. Any other man? You," he said, keeping his gaze on me.

I looked around the cage. Faces of women and ladies and girls who had cried and sobbed and prayed and were weary of all. Their looks told me my time had come and fear crawled into my chest and gave me a sudden sharp pain.

"Come. Out," Merchant said, and then walked close to the cage to open it. Another thing is that I have never seen Merchant open the cage or get as close to it as he did that day, two years ago, and he has never done so again since then. Gimbu always opens the cage. I always cut the fishes.

I walked out of the cage without crying or screaming or holding on to the people in the cage. It was just the pain in my chest that was threatening to take my life as Merchant held me by the neck and dragged me on, to the slab where Gimbu had almost finished cutting.

"Something. About you. Your name?" Merchant asked.

I cleared my throat. "Shakiru."

"Sha. Kiru," he repeated it as if saying it with his own mouth, in his own way, would convince him that I was speaking the truth. "Somethin'bout you. Me believe. You. Useful. No waste."

"Yes," I said. I wasn't thinking. You don't think when you are standing close to a slaughter slab where a human being has just been slaughtered and you could be next.

"You are right, Merchant," Gimbu said, bowing his head slightly as he still does whenever he speaks to Merchant. He had been Merchant's apprentice at the abattoir and they had struggled together to make it in the city until Merchant discovered this business and brought him to this dungeon to continue working for him and be his right hand man. It was Gimbu who later brought the two hefty men who now mount guard at the gate of the dungeon. I don't know their names because neither Merchant nor Gimbu ever call them by name.

Merchant looked across the table to Gimbu, searching his face as if something in it would tell him what he would eventually decide to do with me. "Where. The blood?" he asked Gimbu. Gimbu dropped his machete on the slab and bent beside him, lifting up a small white ceramic bowl containing the thick red fluid he must have collected from the neck of the body on the slab. Merchant stretched his left hand across the slab to collect the bowl from Gimbu without releasing his grip on my neck. Then he brought the bowl across to my face and said, gently, almost in a sexual way, "Drink."

I swallowed painfully past the huge knob in my gullet and it seemed to land straight onto the pain in my chest, cutting it into pieces. I opened my mouth and shut my eyes tight as the cold helm of the ceramic bowl lodged between my lips. I would swallow. I would not let it rest on my tongue. I would do this to save my life. I tasted the blood briefly as I tried to swallow as fast as I could. It tasted like metal in liquid form. It was slightly salty in a way that was liberal, not to be consumed, leaving a rusty taste in the mouth, yet as if you should have more. I didn't want more but when Merchant pressed his fingers deeper into my neck and said, "Everything Shak. Drink. Everything," I opened my eyes to see what was left in the bowl, and then shut my eyes again to prepare for the second attempt. Gimbu just continued with his work, clearing up the slab and putting the fresh parts first in the transparent polythene bag and then in the black ones. He would later tell me that I looked like I was enjoying the taste of the blood that day, and I would simply shake my head, not because of what he said, but for him, for this life he was living for Merchant. I made up my mind never to talk about anything personal with him besides our work for Merchant, especially after the day he told me that Madam was also once just like me. She was a whale that Merchant had pulled out of the cage and decided to make his own, so that she could cook and clean for him and make his bed warm at night and satisfy him with her huge breasts.

I have not had to drink blood since that day. Only in my dreams. Back then, I used to have dreams where I would be in a pool of blood, swimming and swallowing and drowning. Other times, I would see many of the fishes I had slaughtered on the slab carrying their blood in their hands, naked as they came to earth, asking me to drink from their hands. I would refuse, as if I was sure I would join them on the other side if I did. We would struggle and struggle and then I would wake up.

I don't have those dreams anymore. Now all I dream about many times is of a proper life in the city. Somewhere far away. Maybe not in my former community, because by now they must have conducted my funeral with an empty coffin lowered into the ground and they must have almost forgotten about me for good. So showing up there would only complicate things. I would go somewhere else, somewhere distant and start my life all over again, if I ever got out of the dungeon. For now, I would remain loyal, serving Merchant, at least to keep my life, until something happens and I am able to have my life back in my own hands.

***

NOW MERCHANT IS TALKING TO ME, still clenching his fist, about how we must never allow a fish die while still in the aquarium, that every fish is priceless and that we must find out what must have happened in the cage or if anything was wrong with their dinner or if any other fish has any problem. There must never be less than twelve fishes in the aquarium at anytime. Which is another reason I am sure Merchant is angry. The death of the whale leaves us short of one. I look at Merchant a bit closely. His moustache, a faded brown, sitting politely below his chin, almost the same colour as the hair on his large head and the hair just above his wide eyes. Gimbu is apologising to Merchant as if he actually killed the whale. I apologise too, even though I am wondering what the apology is for. Merchant seems happy with the apology, because he releases his fist and reaches for the bottle of gin in front of him. He says, "Go. Check," as if he is talking to the gin as he lifts it to his mouth. Gimbu gets up to leave and I get up to follow him before I hear, "Shak" and I stop in my stride. "Come. Sit."

Merchant doesn't seem happy again. It seems the happiness from our apology vanished as soon as the gin journeyed down his throat into his belly.

"What think happened. Whale?"

I breathe out heavily. "I am not sure, Merchant."

"Not sure. Means then. You know. Something."

"I don't know, Merchant. I am just as confused as you."

"Me. Not confused."

"Yes Merchant."

"Only. Need answers."

"Yes Merchant."

"Fishes never die. In aquarium. Till we ready. Kill."

"Yes Merchant."

"Stop."

"What?"

"Stop. Yes to everything," he says and reaches for his gin again.

"Ok merchant."

"New consignment. Before midnight. Today. Me. No check. Me. Want. Think. You. Check."

"Ok merchant."

"Well done. Shak. You. Great guy," he says as he reclines in his chair as if to begin thinking.

"Thank you Merchant," I say rather too quietly, and then get up to leave.

"Don't go. Go. Gimbu returns."

"Ok Merchant."

"Now. You. Not say. Yes anymore. Now. You say. Ok."

And then rather awkwardly, we both begin to laugh and laugh, maybe because we both know I have never had to stay with him alone like this for this long and it feels really weird.

***

MY EYES WERE ALREADY VERY HEAVY and beginning to close by themselves when our next consignment arrived shortly after midnight. I knew the black bus that drove through the entrance too well already, so I got up quickly from under the big mango tree that serves as shade from the sun during the day, and went in to call Gimbu. He went over to the driver and I began to look into the bus with the small light from the torch in my hands as he and the driver spoke in hushed tones. All the people in the bus, about thirteen of them, were asleep, probably from the effect of the spray, and they had all been blindfolded and their hands tied together behind them. The other man beside the driver got down to open the bus as we began waking up the people one after the other. They became just awake enough to sleep-walk into the cage, one after the other. I searched their faces and counted as they walked. All of them, women, and ladies and a girl. A girl that must have been sixteen or nineteen or anything in between. She had her hair braided and packed backwards, falling just below her shoulders and she wore a tiny ear ring, only one. As I placed my torch close to her blindfolded face, I saw something in her face that made me uneasy. It was as though she could see me even with her blindfold on. Fear crept into my chest when she said, "Where am I?"

"Shhh" I hushed her. "Just move."

"Where am I? Why are my hands and eyes tied?"

I hoped Gimbu and the other men couldn't hear her as we got closer to the cage.

"Just be quiet."

"Please talk to me for heaven's sake? What is happening to me?"

"Girl, you are talking too much," I said to her, and then as if someone pushed me from behind to do so, I leaned towards her ears and whispered, "I will come for you later. Just stay near the cage." I immediately felt the fear in my chest vanish. I didn't know why I had said that. It was as though the words left my mouth of their own will.

"Cage? Oh, Jesus," she spoke louder now. "Oh *kerimama shakabata rankatisa ya ma ka,*" she began to say louder.

"What's that, Shak?" Gimbu said from the entrance of the cage.

"Nothing. This one here is wide awake. I wonder why they don't usually seal their mouths." I saw the driver saying something to Gimbu. I was sure he was trying to defend what I just said.

The girl continued to mutter those strange words to herself, and then she stopped and said, softly, as if someone had told her to, "I will stay by the cage. I will wait for you."

I felt my fear return to my chest.

AFTER I AM SURE GIMBU IS FAST ASLEEP, and snoring loudly, I creep to his side and unstrap the keys to the cage from around his waist. I walk quietly into the cold night and towards the cage. The fear in my chest has moved down to my feet and my hands. I have never opened this cage before and I am not even quite sure why I am doing this. As I put on my torch, I see a figure resting on the metal bars that is the door of the cage. It is the girl with the braided hair. I tap her gently and she comes alive. The others in the cage are all sleeping because there is no sound or movement, except for the birds and insects making quirky sounds in the distance. I take my time to open the door as quietly as I can. I can feel my hands shaking in unison with my feet. It is the fear in them.

I finally open the cage and the girl steps out. I close the cage, leaving the huge padlock from the bars of the cage without locking it. I turn to the girl and my hands stop shaking. I remove her blindfold and then lift my torch a few metres over her face so that we could see each other's faces. She is beautiful, in the way you will speak of a painting. But she looks very tired. Her mouth moves slightly as if she is about to say something and I quietly put my left hand across her mouth and lead her away to the back of the cage. There is a cleared path within the bushes with a chair and a stool. There Merchant used to sit in the early days. Now Gimbu and I sit there when we have nothing serious to do and drink together without talking. I put her blindfold around my neck and gesture to her to sit. I pull the stool closer and sit in front of her.

"What am I doing here?" she asks me.

"What was that language you were speaking?" I ask.

"I was praying. Please what am I doing here, and who are you?"

"You were brought here by some men and this is not a good place to be."

"Please where is this place?"

"You must keep your voice down. I am risking my life by even talking to you."

"Please sir, where is this place?" she says again, trying to whisper this time.

"The Merchant's dungeon." I can see that the fear in my hands and feet have found their way to her face. "What is your name?"

She looks at me, hesitates briefly, and then says, "Joyce."

"Joyce is a sweet name. I am Shakiru, but Merchant and Gimbu call me Shak."

"Who is Merchant? Who is Gimba? Why am I here?"

"Gimbu, not Gimba."

"Mr. Shakiru, what am I doing here with all those people in a prison? Am I going to die? Oh, blood of Jesus."

I reach out to hold her. "You are not going to die. I will not let anything happen to you." I surprise myself. What is this I am doing, I think to myself. "I have to take you back now. But please stop crying. Nothing will happen to you. I will protect you." I begin to return her blindfold to her face and over her eyes. She continues to cry. "Please stop crying Joyce," I say to her as I lead her back to the cage, push her gently into it and lock. I turn around and creep back like a thief into the house.

Gimbu is still snoring. I am sure Merchant is also fast asleep beside madam in his room. I strap the keys back to Gimbu's waist and I go over to my bed to rest my back. As I lay back to get some sleep before morning, I think of Joyce, of her parents, of her school, of her life outside this dungeon. And as I think of her, strangely, a strong sexual urge comes upon me, and I begin to harden between my legs. I try to force it away and sleep, and as I sleep, I dream of Joyce. She is removing my trousers and my pants, and taking me first in her hands, and then in her mouth and soon I am moaning and jerking and spilling my seed all over her hands and her mouth.

***

IT IS GIMBU WHO WAKES ME UP in the morning. Merchant is already out of his room, dressed in his favourite kaftan, the one he only wears on days he knows a lot of politicians would be visiting. I feel the mess in my pants, so I quickly go into the bathroom, and as I go, I hear Merchant ask Gimbu why I am just waking up and if he didn't tell me that we have a lot of work to do today. Gimbu doesn't say anything, so I sigh.

I think about last night a bit before I begin to take off

my clothes. I think about it as something that must never happen again and that must be gone forever. So it is really strange, the sensation that sweeps across my body about a week later when Gimbu comes to me under the mango tree and says, "I know what you did last night," and smiles. I wouldn't be able to respond and I wouldn't be able to close my mouth, but he wouldn't say anything more than that so we both keep looking into the afternoon.

Later, at the slab, I am reluctant. For the first time since the first time I cut a fish apart, I am reluctant. Merchant can see that I am reluctant. I can see it in his face that he is wondering why I am reluctant. Then he walks away, leaving me at the slab. I hear him say, "Customers. Waiting" as he leaves, as if he is talking to himself. I get to work.

***

I DID NOT GO BACK TO THE CAGE to see Joyce again after that day. I tried really hard not to, but I never stopped thinking about her. Until one day, after about a week, the day before Gimbu came to me under the mango tree and said those words.

I had seen Joyce during the day in the cage, and there was something in her eyes that asked me several questions. She wanted to know if I was still going to keep my promise to her. If I had so easily lost interest after that first day. If I would ever come to take her out of the cage again. So, that night, I had unstrapped the keys from Gimbu's side again and gone over to the cage and taken Joyce to the path in the bush behind the cage, just like the first day. She had been a bit more relaxed on this day, subdued, maybe by the reality of the situation and the several others she had seen taken out of the cage never to return again. She even told me a joke, about a woman in the cage who told her it seems I was interested in her, and that she should *gree for me* because that might be the way God planned to get her out of the dungeon, if she agreed to be mine. We both laughed about it, but we both knew there was something in there. Joyce had leaned over on my shoulder as if trying to do what the woman told her and I had held her waist briefly before taking her back to the cage. I killed the woman the next day, but before I began cutting her body apart, I wished I could have asked her what she had seen and what she knew, about Joyce or about me.

***

THE DAY I BEGAN TO FEEL SICK after throwing up just after breakfast, Merchant said I needed a break. He first said I needed a break, and then he said I needed help. He said he used to throw up like that too in the beginning of the business when he was the one doing the cutting and Gimbu was outside mounting guard. He said he would throw up the most when he and Gimbu had to go bury rotten human parts in a big rice bag deep in the bushes because they didn't have so many clients at the time and sometimes goods got stale. He rolled his tongue when he said *stale*. He said I needed to go into the cage and fish out someone that could help me and bring the person to him for initiation. I had brought the only person I thought I needed to him but he said I needed a man, that a young girl couldn't do the job, that women meant trouble and that I should return her and bring a man or a boy. I returned Joyce to the cage and came back. He asked me for the boy and I told him I would be fine without any help. He looked across to madam and they smiled at each other with a frightening oneness. She later gave me medicine in a small bottle which I drank with my eyes closed. It made my sickness vanish.

MERCHANT SAYS THERE IS always this huge demand during electioneering. This is my first election time with him so I don't really know. But now we were running out of fishes, only four left, and neither of our suppliers had brought in any new consignment. Things must be tough out there, I thought. People must have been told to watch their steps and not go out alone in the dark or board buses they were not too sure were safe. Or maybe there was more security presence in the city now because of the coming elections.

MERCHANT COMES OUT OF HIS ROOM, with a towel around his waist and a singlet on, looks towards us and says, "New consignment. Before. Midnight. Thank God." There is a familiar, yet strange vainness to the sound of the word *God* in his mouth. But we are happy. Gimbu and me. We are relieved. I am more relieved because of Joyce. At least she can stay alive for much longer until that elusive miracle happens. I had been worried sick about that.

Later that day, just before midnight, Merchant comes into the open space before the mango tree and I hear him raise his voice for the first time; albeit joyously, "Open! Gate! Consignment." I jump to my feet. I have been sleeping. It doesn't seem like he is coming from within the house. He seems to be coming from deep into the bushes. I assume he is coming from one of his really long meditations, alone in the bushes for several hours before emerging with new ideas, revelations and plans. I had also assumed he was in with madam which is why I am out under the tree at this time. Gimbu is not here. I need to get him so he can open the cage for the consignment. As I begin to walk in the direction of the house, I hear Merchant's voice again. "Where. You?"

"To get Gimbu, sir. He needs to open the cage."

"Leave. Gimbu. Me. Give you. Key. Special consignment. Together," he said, as if he knew something I didn't know.

I go towards him and together we begin to go towards the gate.

"Much. Fishes. In cage," he says to me, staring at the ground before us.

"I think they are four left, sir."

"Go. Check. Sure."

"Ok Merchant." I begin to walk away before I hear his last word.

Just as I get to the cage and my eyes meet Joyce's and the three others' in the cage, I hear the familiar sound of the black bus coming in through the gate. But as I turn to look towards the gate, it is not the two men that I know that are stepping out of the bus. These men are different. They are dressed in black. So many of them, carrying guns and running out of the bus in different directions.

Merchant also sees them, so he turns around immediately as if to begin to run but they open fire before he can even move. And just as their bullets hit him and I imagine he would fall to the ground, lifeless, he disappears. He simply vanishes, as if something in the bullets had enabled him to. One of the policemen mouths a curse. I hear more shots. The two men at the gate lay dead. Gimbu still hadn't stepped out of the house. He must have vanished too. It must be something the both of them know how to do. A secret they hadn't quite trusted me enough to share with me. And I thought my feelings for Joyce was the only secret in this dungeon.

Now a policeman is pointing his gun in my direction as he walks towards me screaming, "Hands up!" I am bolted out of my thoughts by his voice, and by two of his colleagues who have rushed into the house and were now leading two people - Gimbu, and madam - out of the house, naked, handcuffed. I am about to choke. One of the policemen shakes his head as he speaks to the others coming towards him, "*You no go believe. These ones dey inside dey fuck sef.*" Something forms in my throat. I spit out saliva. I look to the policeman holding the gun in front of me, and I immediately begin to go towards him, shouting, "Thank God o! Thank God you people are finally here o!" He looks at me weirdly, cocks his gun and screams, "Stand back!

Don't move!" I can hear Joyce's voice in the cage speaking that strange language. I keep running towards the policeman. Then, quite suddenly, I feel a sharp searing pain in my chest, and then I hear a loud gunshot, then nothingness.

Uncle Solo

UNCLE SOLO LOOKS nothing like the fifty-something years he has spent on earth. He tries very hard to look thirty, and he succeeds. Mostly. He tries hard to look and act like he owns the world and that he could get whatever he wanted at any time; the fattest girls, the fattest beer mugs or even the very expensive ashen powder that sustains his life.

Uncle Solo is my elder brother, but calling him *Brother Solo* would be totally out of place. Not just because no one else in this entire area calls him that, but the age difference between him, my younger brother, Edwin, and I is simply too much. The reason is that after our parents gave birth to Uncle Solo, they had to wait several years – I cannot remember how many years exactly now – and pray, and fast and call on the God of Hannah, before they were able to give birth to Edwin and me. That meant that Uncle Solo was the only child for a very long time and he enjoyed all the privileges and pampering that came with being the first and only child of a wealthy man, a very successful oil dealer with about five petrol stations scattered around town.

Today though, there is only one petrol station left. And that one is the only one Uncle Solo is yet to sell. The only reason he has not sold it, I think, is because our father had already handed over the management of that station to one of his friends under a lease agreement which, if I am to believe what I was told, will last for about thirty years or so. So Uncle Solo has to really wait before he can sell that one.

One after the other, we have watched all the other property our father left us disappear before our very eyes, and in exchange, we have been compensated with regular viewing of Uncle Solo's sexual escapades with different shades of women, through the keyhole of his room. Sometimes, when he wants to really feel and prove that he is still thirty, he engages two or three women at a time. Mostly portly women. He has success-fully polluted my eyes and my mind, because now I know how to do things I never even should have heard about in my life.

We've also been compensated with regular drama. Uncle Solo no longer has a car, after he sold off the last car that was left because he needed to sniff on the whitish powder that keeps him alive. The only person who had the powder at the time had demanded for eight hundred thousand naira for the size of powder that was nothing more than the twenty naira garri with which myself and Edwin ate our beans on privileged days. Uncle Solo saw nothing else that was worth that amount to offer, except the 2005 Honda Accord car.

So since then, he became used to trekking, and we also became used to seeing him come home drunk. Whenever he was getting dressed to go to the beer parlour, he would say, to no one in particular, that at the beer parlour, drinks could never be scarce even if you didn't have a kobo because there would always be people who just won *Baba Ijebu money* and would come there to 'declare' for everybody. Besides, there were also people whose drinking habits he had personally financed in his hey days, so this was the time for him to enjoy the harvest of his seeds. People who leave home for work very early in the morning in our area have also become used to picking Uncle Solo up from gutters where he often sleeps comfortably. They used to care initially, and they would come to knock on our door and ask us with pitiful faces to come carry our brother out of the gutter. But they don't care anymore because if Uncle Solo was not in the gutter, we would probably find him sleeping at the gate beside his alcohol laden vomit. Or, in his saner days, he would have been arrested by the vigilante people the night before and be threatening them in his usual way, asking if they did not know; first, the son of who he was, and then who he himself was.

"I will destroy you!" he would say, pointing his middle finger at his object of anger.

Once, he told us the story of how he almost *destroyed* a policeman who dared to stop him at a check-point when those checkpoints still used to exist all over town. He had been smoking Indian hemp inside the Honda Accord and must have also been drunk. He didn't tell us that, but I know that it is the way Uncle Solo is. The policeman asked my brother to roll down the glass of his car, and this is what I think must have happened, because Uncle Solo's version couldn't have been the truth. The stench of alcohol, and *igbo* coming from his car must have been a rude shock to the policeman.

"Park well! Park well! Driving under the influence! Park!" That is how those police people talk.

Uncle Solo could not have obeyed, because he does not obey anybody. He told us that he laughed - a drunken laugh - pulled out his mobile phone, stared hard at the policeman's uniform and then called his name out – "Kingsley O.N" before dialling the Commissioner's phone number. He has a lot of friends in high places because of the foolish favours he has rendered and lavish monies he has spent during his lifetime.

"Edem-Edem! Commissioner Edem! The only man who knows where to locate the Garden of Eden. *How you dey, how life, how pikin, how all ya girlfriends?*" he must have asked rapidly in his usual way and then laughed another drunken laugh to prove to the policeman that himself and this commissioner were really best of friends. "*All these ya boys wey you put for road dey disturb me o. I dey smoke my igbo jeje for my car, he say make I park under the influence. I go jam am o!*" Then he must have put the phone on loudspeaker, so the policeman could hear the commissioner's response. That's how he got out of most difficult situations in those days.

Now that the reality of our hunger and poverty is really beginning to bite hard, we are no longer interested in the regular drama or his stories. Sometimes, we even ignore the keyhole when Uncle Solo is busy, but we still leave our ears wide open to listen to the moans and strange noises that come from his room. This is the only house left of the four different houses our parents left for us before death took them away suddenly in that fatal motor accident. I don't like to remember it, even though they were very old. I was very young then.

I picked up music along the line when there was really nothing else to do after I managed to finish school. Several times, I have asked Uncle Solo to help raise some money for my demo, but each time I ask, he would ask me to sing my song for him so that he could tell me if it was something Nigerians would love to listen to. His idea of Nigerians, I'm sure, is his friends at the beer parlour. I would summon all the courage I could and sing him *Ololufe,* my best song at that time. It was also the only song I had composed. He would laugh, that stupid drunken laugh, and say something about how if a child's hands is yet to grasp the dagger, he shouldn't ask about the death that killed his father, and that I should go and wait for my time and continue practising.

Well, one day, something happened. Something strange.

Uncle Solo woke us up very early in the morning and began to speak in a way I had never seen him speak before – in a calm, gentle tone. He started with several questions.

"Una like as everything dey happen for this house?"

Myself and Edwin shared a curious look.

"Una dey chop well?"

I wanted to tell him that we all knew this and that he

should go straight to the point. But as we usually say here, *dem no born me well to talk that kain thing*, so I kept my mouth shut.

"*Una dey make progress?*"

I wanted to remind him that he wasn't making much progress himself.

"*Una no want make we move forward?*"

He was no longer waiting for us to shake our heads to his questions. He went on and on and then said the one that got us worried.

"*I don check all these things well and I don decide say, na prayer we need for this house...*"

I and Edwin sat up without looking at each other.

"*...and I don decide say we go fast for three days.*"

That wouldn't be difficult; we 'fasted' most days, anyway.

He handed me a clean two hundred naira note and asked me to go and buy packets of candles – red, white and yellow. I wanted to tell him that those colours might not be available and that one packet of candle was one hundred and twenty naira, and the money would not be enough. But I didn't want to spoil the holy mood that Uncle Solo was in, because I was sure that somewhere underneath this newness, was the Uncle Solo who would 'destroy you' for every slightest provocation.

As I ran to get the candles, to avoid missing out on any further drama, my thoughts also picked pace. I began to doubt the entire setting. It seemed like something those *yahoo* boys call *format*. Why would Uncle Solo suddenly turn born-again, overnight? Did he have a dream in which Jesus Christ suddenly appeared to him and told him we needed prayers?

I thought the fact that Uncle Solo suddenly realised that we needed prayers was the biggest shock of the morning, I didn't expect what I heard when I got back home with the candles. I bought just two sticks of candle per colour and wrapped them together in a black nylon, so I could have some change to keep.

"I don decide say I go go mountain go do my own prayer and fasting, because I no want any distraction for here."

Now Edwin and I looked at each other again. I could see laughter threatening to burst forth from his face. *Dem no born am well to laugh.*

Swiftly, Uncle Solo went into his room and some minutes later, he came out bathed and dressed in a white garment. He held a big bible and put the candles and a bottle of water into a polythene bag and started walking towards the door.

"Unkuul...please give us chop mo-o-neey," Edwin stammered.

As if he had prepared for the question, he turned around and screamed, *"Wetin una wan take chop money do? Person wey dey fast dey chop?"*

"Unkuul, make I help you carry these things reach bus-stop," I offered.

"No worry. I no need help. Make nobody follow me o!"

That was when my suspicion grew. On a normal day, Uncle Solo would be the one to order you to carry his things and follow him. Why was he insisting that nobody should follow him? I smelt a very big rat, so I decided to follow him.

Uncle Solo got outside our house, looked to the right and to the left and then began to walk down the road towards the bus-stop. I followed him, maintaining a safe distance. I had told Edwin to take care of the house because I needed to get to the bottom of this. Uncle Solo got to the bus-stop and simply kept walking. He didn't stop to join the people waiting to board buses to their various destinations. I also noticed that people looked at him in a strange way and left the road for him as though he had a contagious disease. I was sure some who may have known him wouldn't have been able to recognise him. My curiosity was really beginning to grow. I began to think of several possibilities.

Maybe Uncle Solo was going crazy. No, I thought, after all, he was already crazy. This had to be something serious.

Maybe he was going to begin preaching in buses in a location where nobody really knew who he was, and so he would be able to deceive people and collect money from them in the name of 'supporting the ministry'. There were many of such bus preachers around town these days, giving the genuine ones a bad name. I tried to imagine Uncle Solo preaching in a bus, but I couldn't. It just didn't seem right.

Or, maybe he was really a changed man now; maybe he was even going to become a pastor. No. He couldn't. I couldn't even imagine Uncle Solo as a pastor. He would be the lousiest clergyman ever. A typical prayer session in his church would be loaded with several strange terms and concepts, especially the *destroying* of demons. No demon would even listen to Uncle Solo if he were to try to cast out any. The demon would only have to remind him of all his past sins and atrocities and then ask him, "Jesus I know, Paul I know, but who are you?" Thinking about my Uncle Solo as a pastor made me remember a certain pastor with long beards and a bald head, who they said set fire on his church members for fornicating. Uncle Solo can *destroy* people like that.

I was beginning to get tired of walking, but Uncle Solo kept walking very quickly, as though he had an appointment to keep. I struggled to keep pace with him, still maintaining a safe distance, although he never looked back. After a really long while, we were greeted by the noise of bus conductors and travellers at the inter-state bus park. Then Uncle Solo suddenly vanished amidst the crowd of people. I cursed and kicked my carelessness for letting him get out of sight. But I had come too far to back down. I would wait.

ABOUT TWENTY MINUTES and several pure water sachets later, I suddenly saw a frame that looked just like my brother emerging from one of the several spaces between rows of buses. "This can't be Uncle Solo," I thought to myself. He looked completely different. Like thirty. No white garment. No bible. No candles.

He wore a white Polo t-shirt. It looked original, because Edwin always says that if you see a Polo t-shirt where the man was either chasing the horse or the horse was chasing the man, then it was a fake one. He said the fakest one was the one where the man and the horse would be pursuing the stick. The man on Uncle Solo's t-shirt was sitting on the horse and he held the stick in his hand. Uncle Solo also wore a pair of blue jeans and white trainers to go with his shirt. He looked stunning. My mouth formed an O shape as I watched him raise his right hand slightly to find out the time on what looked like a very expensive wrist-watch. Then he brought out his mobile phone and made a call before hurriedly walking towards the road. I followed him, making sure not to lose him this time.

He stood just by the road and soon, a taxi parked and a lady alighted from the cab. She was no ordinary lady. Slim, fair-skinned and tall. Not like the fat ones Uncle Solo usually brought home. She looked like she had just stepped out of the cover of a fashion magazine. She had to be a model or an actress or something like that. Then she hugged and kissed my brother, right there on the road. I licked my lips. This kind of girl shouldn't even agree to date Uncle Solo, let alone kiss him in public. Something was certainly amiss.

I quickly hid behind one of the buses as Uncle Solo turned around after receiving the lady's luggage from the taxi driver and paying the fare. He began to walk towards one of the long luxury buses holding on tightly to the lady, while the bus conductors hurried towards them to collect the luggage. The bus was almost filled with passengers.

But I still didn't understand it. Where was Uncle Solo going? Holiday? Why did he need to lie to us to get out of the house? After all, he had often left home several times for days without having to explain to us where he was going or where he had been. Or was this a permanent move? Was he eloping with this *Omalicha*, or is she the one who has been collecting all the money from the sale of our father's properties? Maybe he was really leaving us for good now and would therefore have us believe that he was on some mountain somewhere praying for us. My head began to ache. I called for another sachet of pure water.

What would happen to Edwin and me now? What about my dream of becoming a musician? How would we even feed?

As I thought hard and long, trying to figure things out, I did not notice when the bus began to make its way out of the park, because suddenly the lyrics for a song began to come together in my mind. I sang it out to myself while I bent my head slightly, pouring the cold water from the sachet onto my head:

> *Uncle Solo solo, I see you when you*
> *want to enter Marcopolo, bros,*
> *You dey wear Polo polo, you think say*
> *I be mumu abi I don kolo...*
> *Uncle Solo solo, I see you when you*
> *want to enter Marcopolo, chai!*
> *Bros, you dey wear Polo polo, I see you*
> *when you want to follow Tolo tolo...*

I repeated the lyrics several times until a broad smile lit up my face. I loved the sound of it. My legs began to move too as the beats formed in my mind and I made sounds with my mouth. Maybe I can even sing it one day and it will be a big hit and I will become a big music star. Maybe this is the way God wants to take us away from poverty, away from the hardship Uncle Solo has put us through all these years.

I felt a hand tap on my right shoulder all of a sudden, and when I looked up, it was Edwin.

"Edwin," I almost screamed, "What are you doing here?"

"Where is-is he?"

"Uncle Solo?" I asked.

He nodded, he was panting. He must have been running.

"He is in that bus," I said, pointing in the direction where the bus was and then noticed it had left the park and was now gathering speed on the major road. "Why are you here?"

"He cannot go."

"What?"

"There are some men in the house, they are locking up the house, they said Uncle Solo has sold the house to them and we should pack out immediately."

"What?!"

Without saying anything else to each other, Edwin and I took off our slippers and dashed off in the direction of the park entrance. We ran after the Marcopolo bus, shouting "Stop! Stop!" as fast as our legs and hungry voices could carry us.

Flight Partner

I STEPPED OUT OF THE TAXI into the surprising cool of the Lagos airport that evening feeling helpless, especially after the cab driver brought out my luggage – two big bags - from the boot and drove off. At least the bags were one less than I came with on my flight from Houston which had earned me extra luggage charges. I had distributed all the cheap shoes, t-shirts, perfumes and toiletries I came with to all my nieces and nephews who had come to greet their 'Aunty Joy from America'.

I was beginning to feel like it was a mistake insisting on coming to the airport alone. I had insisted because I didn't want any of those elaborate departure hugs and kisses from family members that often drew attention. And I certainly didn't want my mother taking the opportunity of the time it might take to check my luggage in to begin talking to me again about how there were plenty Nigerian men, even those from our place, back in Houston that I could find and hold on to and bring home the next time I was coming to Nigeria, as though husbands were apples you could simply pluck off trees. There would be no next time; I had assured myself after she said that.

My luggage now seemed like a burden, and just as I wondered how I was going to get them as far as the departure area all by myself, two men walked up to me. They were wearing uniform vests which suggested that they were some form of airport officials. Without the vests though, they could well have been touts, judging by the rest of their appearance.

"Departure? We'll help you ma," they said in unison and then without waiting for my response, picked up each of my bags as though they were weightless grocery baskets.

"Oh, thanks, that's nice of you," I grinned.

"You go find us something when we reach there," one of them said as they began to move.

"Oh," I sighed.

THE SECURITY MEN AT THE ENTRANCE of the departure hall were interrogating a couple when I got there. It looked like the husband was the one travelling being the only one brandishing a passport at the security guards and they were expecting him to 'settle' them to let his wife in. It was a good thing no one came with me after all. How much would I have had to pay to let Mama, Ikedi, Naomi and the maid in? I moved to the second entrance.

"Madam, safe journey," the officer in black and army green said after he examined my passport absent-mindedly, and then added, "anything for us?"

I dragged my bags in without a word and began to scan the hall for the airline check-in counter. I knew it would certainly take some time to get checked in at any airport, let alone a Nigerian airport, but nothing prepared me for the queue of people and luggage I saw waiting to be checked in on the Air France queue. It was scary, to say the least. It reminded me instantly of the days of queuing to fetch water whenever the tanks were empty and water was still being pumped at the hostels back in Queens College before I moved to the U.S for university. It sent shivers down my spine, but I didn't let the shivers stop me from practically racing to the end of the seemingly endless queue before it got even longer.

"Is this the Air France queue?" I asked the lady in front of me.

"Yeah, Continental Airline, to Toronto," she responded.

"Ok." I understood her response. Air France and Continental Airline had some form of partnership where they combined their passengers. The flight would make a stop-over at Houston where I would disembark while the others would later be put on a connecting flight to Toronto.

"So, you live in Toronto too?"

"Houston," I said, dragging my second bag in line.

"You know I haven't been to Nigeria since I was four. What about you?"

"Since High School."

I began to look around just to distract myself. I certainly wasn't here to make friends or engage in chit-chat or get a flight partner for that matter. I noticed the couple I had seen at the entrance earlier. They were on the adjourning queue for South-Africa Airways. I followed the trail of the queue and almost couldn't see the end of it as it bent out of view. I wondered how that had happened in such a short time, and how the couple had gotten themselves into the queue. That certainly had to be it. They must have jumped the queue to be where they were because they certainly weren't there when I got in line. I looked at them closely as the lady leaned towards the man, whispering something. I noticed a bulge in her stomach. Then almost impulsively, I looked at her fingers, searching. No rings. I cleared my throat. Or did she take her ring off deliberately the way they say some pregnant women like to do? I cross-examined the man's hands. No rings too. They suddenly didn't look married anymore. I should have known. I thought they said women in Nigeria don't get pregnant outside wedlock, that it is those of us who live abroad that do such things. I didn't realise the lady next to me on the queue had asked me another question until I felt her arm tap.

"What?" I asked.

"Thinking of something, someone?"

"Oh, no, just wondering why the queue for South Africa is so long."

"I guess it's easier for Nigerians to get visas to South Africa, being an African country."

"I guess."

"So, you live in America?"

"Yes. Houston," *I said that before, right?* I wanted to add.

"What brought you home?"

Home? I hesitated and searched the lady's face, taking in her details - light blue eyes, possibly from contact lenses, full eye lashes and long eye brows, a small nose and full lips emphasised by red lipstick. "I came to see my mother."

"Oh! Me too! I came to see my parents, and they couldn't stop talking about getting a husband even after not seeing me for all these years, as if husbands are groceries you could pick up from the grocery store."

"Really? My mum too."

We laughed.

"I'm Joy."

"Rose."

And with that, I disposed of my initial scepticism about this blue-eyed lady and we began to talk. We talked about men. About Nigerian men, the ones living in Nigeria and the ones abroad, their differences and similarities. We talked about what men had in common - women, cars, wrist-watches, lying and cheating. We talked a lot about the last two. Blue Eyes had an interesting experience to share. She had travelled from Toronto to see her Nigerian boyfriend who lived in Washington, and whose tuition and accommodation she was paying for by working three jobs, only to meet him giving his male flatmate head. That was how she said it. I looked around, embarrassed, trying to be sure no one else heard her.

"Men!" I concluded.

"Even the cookie is no longer enough, now they want bananas. I'm certainly done with them! Like done!" she flashed her right hand across her neck twice when she said 'done'.

I noticed a slight squabble developing in front of us at the counter and it provided a welcome diversion. One of the airport officials was holding out his ID card to an angry looking man who kept saying, "No way! This is unacceptable!" We would later find out that the 'official' had tried to smuggle in someone who had just arrived and place her right at the head of the queue. In the meantime, the angry man who was apparently acting on behalf of the rest of us on the queue was insisting that such deviousness would not be tolerated.

"This man doesn't know that some of these guys feed and live on this," Blue Eyes said.

"Shouldn't they rather find proper jobs?" I asked.

"Where are the jobs?"

"Shey," I said, surprising myself.

We continued to watch the drama unfold as others began to add their voice to the unfolding drama and soon the official was overwhelmed into submission.

ABOUT AN HOUR AND SEVERAL EPISODES LATER, myself and Blue Eyes were finally at the counter, dragging our bags unto the Customs table to be checked.

"What is this?" the female officer asked, wielding my vibrator in full public glare.

"A toy!" I snatched it and tucked it back in between my clothes. Blue Eyes giggled.

"*Which kain toy be this one*," the officer said, not giving up. She pulled it out again from between my clothes.

"Adult toy, officer," Blue Eyes offered. "Stop embarrassing the lady."

"*You for talk say na that kain toy*," she winked. I was livid.

IT WAS ONE OF THE SHORTEST FLIGHTS I had ever been on, because I slept off almost immediately. When I woke up, Blue Eyes was saying something I couldn't hear.

She wrote her phone number on a card she pulled out of her wallet and slipped it into my cleavage. Just as I pulled it out and quickly looked over her shoulder to be sure nobody saw us, she squeezed my breasts hurriedly and said, "firm." I swallowed hard. I was too shocked for words.

Later, after I picked up my luggage and we hugged goodbye, she grabbed my butt, squeezed and whispered, "I'll be expecting your call girl."

I immediately knew what I would do with Blue Eyes' phone number once I got to the closest trash bin. She must think I am also done with men simply because they lie and cheat and I keep a vibrator. If only she knew.

A NOTE ABOUT THE AUTHOR

'Seun Salami is a writer and editor. He is the Head of Publishing at Bookvine. He has an MSc in Mass Communication from the University of Lagos. 'Seun has authored two short story collections, *The Son of Your Father's Concubine* and *The Sex Life of a Lagos Mad Woman* and a novella, *The Young Shall Grow*.

ACKNOWLEDGEMENTS

I am sincerely grateful to God and highly indebted to all the people who made these stories and by extension this book, possible.

I am grateful to Moyo, my editor at Bookvine, for her relentless efforts and to Joy, my editor-at-large for providing a fresh perspective.

I am grateful to Taiwo for our precious friendship that kept me sane many times.

I am grateful to Bayo, for the brilliant photographs, the official trailer of this book and choosing one of the stories for his annual documentary feature film.

I am deeply grateful to my wonderful parents for being so supportive of my writing all these years and my siblings - Sanya and Kemi - for their love and understanding. And to Dorcas, the love of my life, for weathering the storm.

PREVIOUSLY PUBLISHED STORIES

An abridged version of the title story *The Sex Life of a Lagos Mad Woman* was first published on YNaija.com

Our Pastor is Hooked on Porn and Me, *The Lump in my Celibate Throat* (as 'The Lump in Your Celibate Throat'), *Aminu Suya* (as 'Flesh and Blood on Aminu-suya's Knife'), *Our New Neighbour's Wife* and *Uncle Solo* were first published in slightly different forms on YNaija.com and on SeunWrites.com, the author's blog.

Uncle Solo was inspired by a song titled, 'Uncle Solo' by Wale Waves - Nigerian recording artiste and the song performer for the award winning movie soundtrack of Kunle Afolayan's Figurine (Araromiire).

Flight Partner was first published in Explore Travel Magazine (2nd Issue, 2014)

ALSO BY 'SEUN SALAMI

The Son of Your Father's Concubine

The Young Shall Grow